Spectra
and the Magic Sled of Nir

Jake Smith

DEDICATION

This book was written for the team at Leica Morrisville.
OCTMonth.com

ACKNOWLEDGMENTS

I owe endless thanks to my editor.
Thank you Mom!

1

The door creaks open and a sneaky set of eyes peer out. When she hears only silence, Spectra plots her next move. *Be sly*, she tells herself.

With a gentle touch, she pulls the handle further until her slim frame can squeeze through. She eases her bare foot down, ball first, across the carpet. The door down the hall to her brother's room remains firmly shut with the light off.

Her breathing eases as she moves down the hall toward the staircase. The handrail feels cool to her touch. She knows the fourth step makes a noise like the howl of a miserable wailing cat, so she sets her left foot down against the wall of that step.

Silence.

She exhales.

As she turns the corner to the kitchen, she glances back over her shoulder. There's nothing behind her. The lights are still off.

Spectra can smell the scrumptious cookies on the counter. Their sugary, confectionary aroma seeps through the top of the large porcelain jar, wafting far and wide from fridge to couch.

She approaches and then ever-so carefully grabs the lid by the knob. Her long fingers gently grasp and remove the top, setting it down safely on the counter.

The sight is glorious. There are layers of cracked brown sugar with a smattering of solid chocolate chunks. It won't be a warm cookie anymore, but it will still retain the soft, chewy texture that Spectra loves. Cookies are underrated. That gooey center will be pure bliss if she can make it back up to her room unnoticed. *Don't rush*, she reminds herself.

Ever the aspiring ninja, Spectra re-tops the jar. There's a clink that she can't avoid.

She holds her breath for a count of eight.

Nobody heard the noise.

Spectra pirouettes back toward the staircase with tender steps. Her zephyr-like tip-toeing glides back up to her room. She turns and closes the door with a soft hand, leaving only an imperceptible click as she releases the doorknob.

She made it.

Spectra savors the bounty for her skilled extraction as she sinks her front teeth into the cookie slowly. It's magnificent. She stops holding back and devours the rest of the cookie before she can think about the world beyond the door to her room.

The next morning, she awakes to find that her crime has gone unnoticed.

Her brother, Liam, is down at the kitchen table eating a bowl of multi-colored sugar-crusted cereal flakes. He barely looks up as she enters the room.

Spectra's mother is making fried eggs with way too much pepper.

"Don't get your hopes up, Spectra. These eggs are for me."

Spectra is miffed.

She is thirteen and has to deal with her parents and their grumpy mood. A fog moved into their village a little over a month ago and ever since then, people have become increasingly bitter. They act nasty toward each other and friendships have started to fray. It's not obvious why the fog is causing everybody to become unfriendly, but she suspects that if people could see the stars in the sky again, they might not think they are so important in this vast universe. The constellations of Corvus, Ara, Scorpius, Draco, Ursa Minor, and Ursa Major get obscured well below the peaks of Everest and Mount Blanc.

"I wasn't planning on it, Mother," Spectra says.

Spectra grabs an apple from the counter and some cherry yogurt from the fridge. Her breakfast is going to be light today. She returns to her room to pack her bag with the food so that she can quickly escape out for an adventure.

Spectra's mother, Ruby Morris, sits down at the white oak table to eat breakfast with Liam.

"What do you have planned for today, Liam?"

"There's a giant chestnut tree past the old church that I want to climb," he said. "And Mason said he found a map showing there's something in the tree or maybe a hole in the ground with buried treasure."

"Don't get hurt. I don't want a bloody kid to deal with."

"Mommy... can I bring a cookie with me out to the tree?"

Ruby sighs. "Go grab one."

Liam opens the cookie jar. He can't help but notice there's very clearly a cookie missing. There were only three in there last night and now there are two, which is too small of a number to have a missing treat go unnoticed.

"I think a cookie disappeared."

"Who stole the cookie from the cookie jar?" asked Ruby.

"Not me!" wailed Liam. "It was Spectra."

An unbalanced anger starts to build up in Ruby. The fog clouds her ability to control her temperament. Her ears turn red and her jaw slides forward. She storms out of the room and finds Hugh, Spectra's Dad.

Hugh and Ruby go straight to their daughter's room and knock on the door.

When Spectra swings it open, the door catapults a crumb of cookie from the carpet. Her eyes widen as it lands on Hugh's foot. She is caught.

"What do you think you are doing?" Hugh booms.

The walls are trembling in fear. His voice never used to get this loud.

"It's just a cookie, Dad."

"We were saving that cookie for a special occasion," he says, seeking a reason why he's so upset, "and now you ruined it because of your *appetite*. What do you have to say for yourself?"

"I'm sorry," Spectra replies.

"You're grounded!" he beams.

Spectra's parents storm away. Spectra closes the door. Her bedroom becomes her cell for the day.

The room feels lonely. It feels constricting. There's a giant poster of Ziyi Zhang from *House of Flying Daggers* on the wall. Looking at Ziyi makes Spectra feel a little less alone. She knows it's only a poster.

A perfectly good Saturday, ruined, she thinks.

Sitting on her bed, Spectra starts picking at the stitching of her comforter. She glances at the night stand and sees her alarm clock displaying that the day would be exceedingly long.

The fog is causing this angst. Her parents never used to be this short-tempered. They are still loving parents, but have also become frustrated, selfish, and despotic. She's scared of Hugh now. Even Ruby seemed ill-tempered, getting so upset at breakfast. Their judgment is impaired by the fog. They can no longer see past their own noses. Like the rest of the adults in the village of Ivv, they have lost the ability to empathize. The town is on edge;

something has to give.

Spectra decides that she must do something. She is compelled to fix the issue. She had learned early on that if a girl waits for the world to fix itself she ends up disappointed and disgusted.

The fog must go.

But how does one remove fog?

And that is the crux of the issue. Without a clear plan, the adults sit by and do nothing. They are content being malcontents. The issues they deal with are all within a two-foot radius.

Liam wasn't going to do it; of that she is sure. Her brother would just make things worse, like he always does. Like with the cookies. *Why couldn't he just keep his stupid little mouth shut?*

Spectra must create the change. She alone must lift the fog from her village, lift her village from the fog. Too long has the issue gone unaddressed. If she sat in her room one more day there was no knowing how perturbed her parents would become. Her parents must become nice again and only lifting the fog will allow for it.

She must sneak out of the house, clear the fog, and return, all before dinner.

Failure would mean a village in dispirit, a house in dismay, and her own life in disarray. The thought alone was distressing.

She must succeed. And she must not get caught in the act.

2

As an aspiring ninja, the ability to move freely is more important to Spectra than the fear of getting caught. She dons her favorite bright red pleated skirt with pockets and her fitted white baseball T with the red rings on the sleeves. It's reckless to wear red instead of midnight shadow black, but if somebody sees her face, it wouldn't matter what she was wearing. Maybe they wouldn't suspect her of being up to anything in such an intense color, she figures. Maybe she could *skirt* right past their unsuspecting glances. Spectra puts her hair in a ponytail.

She starts packing her daypack. In addition to the apple and cherry yogurt from downstairs, she adds some hidden munchies from her room. There's a granola bar and some fruity gummies. She stuffs them both in the main pouch. She throws a bottle of water in the bag as well and decides she's good. The backpack feels good when she puts it on. It feels better when she repacks it with the water on bottom.

Spectra is ready for adventure. Her veins fill with anticipation.

She knows how she must start her adventure. This isn't the first time she snuck out of the house. Her bedroom is on the second story. There's a wide window looking out on an alley and the neighbor next door. She opens it and removes the screen. As she steps out onto the roof, the tread on her boots grips the shingles well. She closes the window behind her to block the wind and cool air from entering.

With careful balance, she takes small steps. There's a drain pipe below the gable that makes for a good grip. It's surprisingly sturdy; sturdy enough to act like a fireman's pole.

Spectra's boots hit the dirt with a soft thud. Without the sun poking through, it hasn't dried out since the last rain. The dirt is mostly mud. Small splatters hit her calves.

She holds for a breath.

There's no stirring in the house. The yard is clear. She is free.

The center of the village of Ivv has a cobblestone plaza with wrought iron benches and a yellow-trimmed wooden gazebo. Back when the sun used to poke through, there were flower beds bursting with a rainbow of colors. The weeping willows formerly provided shade. Swanson Plaza, as it is known, is surrounded by bright stucco row shops with smooth white columns holding up rolling arches. The town's people are dreary, but the wrens are chirping and flying among their favorite branches.

Swanson Plaza is the first place that Spectra thinks to go. It's quiet this morning. The daunting task reaches top of mind.

How do you make fog go away? she thinks to herself. *You can't just ask it nicely. You can't shoo it away or threaten it. Some tasty snacks wouldn't trick it to leave, would they? Have we tried baking snacks to placate the fog? It might like ice cream with rainbow sprinkles.*

Spectra climbs up into the gazebo in the center of her hometown and stands straight. It's a high vantage point. She rotates slowly, trying to see something – anything – in the distance that would give her an idea. Quarter-turn, then half-turn, then all the way back around.

Nothing.

Her shoulders slump.

She pulls the apple out of her backpack and starts chomping away. The chewing seems louder in the gazebo. Spectra thinks at a louder volume. Each bite arrests her thoughts.

Does the fog have an odor? she thinks with sniffing nostrils. *Maybe there's a hint of old workshop machinery. There could be a musk of charcoal briquettes. And was that oatmeal raisin?*

Spectra is at a loss. Anxiety finds her. How is she supposed to go on her quest if she doesn't know what she's even looking for? The day is not starting out with a strong lead.

Don't be discouraged, she tells herself. *If it was easy, even a little brother would have done it by now. Important goals are indefinite and onerous.*

The big words rebuild her confidence.

Dew beads up on blades of grass. The green lightens by two shades.

Mornings can be the best time of day. Spectra loves the refreshing mist on her face and in her hair, even if the rest of her village hates it. She feels tougher for it. Pirates always have mist in their faces. Some of the adults she knows sound like pirates before they have their coffee. Or, at least, they sound like sailors. *Maybe drinking coffee makes one allergic to swashbuckling.*

The quiet breeds hope. By midday, a cacophony of aggravating sounds closes off the possibility that adventure may still come. Early morning bird chirping has the opposite effect.

An old man is walking by. His shirt is tattered. Is he a pirate?

His beard smells of cinnamon and mold.

"Hello sir. Do you know what caused this fog?"

Spectra asks.

"I bet it's that *darn-splattin'* village a coupl'a miles down the road. They're ain't always up to doin' no good o'er there," the old man replied with a grumble. Some spit escapes on the hard consonants.

Spectra notices that old men often blame other villages for their problems.

"But how do they make the fog?" Spectra asks.

"Ain't a *darn-splattin'* fog machine, then I ain't know squat."

He doesn't seem happy. Is grumps always a curmudgeon or is this caused by the fog? What could possibly be so bad in his life that would cause a man to complain so much? He should go on adventures! He should become a pirate if he isn't one already!

"Why would they do such a thing? It's just making people get upset," Spectra says.

"What you thinkin' I am? A libary? I bet it's a cockamamie scheme they doin' a raise the taxes again on us."

A library! Yes, of course, Spectra thinks. She'll start her search there first.

"Maybe they are," she says.

She cocks her head a little bit and continues, "Thank you very much. You have been most helpful, old man."

The old man just swats his wrist and grumbles as he waddles away.

Spectra's mission has a next stop.

She leaps up and strides toward the library.

3

Spectra enters Fujimoto Library through the large double doors.

It's quiet.

There's so much knowledge here, she thinks. *What kind of book can I find that will teach me about fog? My parents are oppressed by the weight and thickness of the low cloud. Let's see...*

She starts off by looking for the meteorology section. She finds books about volcanos and lightning and volcanic lightning, but her local government doesn't fund the library like they should, so she can't find one about fog.

There's a selection of history books too. She finds tomes on the dust bowl on the bottom shelf and a military textbook about the fog of war on the top shelf. They aren't what she needs.

She finds *The Buried Giant* in the fiction section. After scanning through the description, she decides to read a few pages. It catches her interest, but she realizes it won't help.

Spectra gets distracted in a section on parenting. Unfortunately, all the practical advice is about how parents can deal with their kids. She needs a book on how kids can help their struggling parents. Surely, she isn't the only girl with parent issues.

She walks around looking for the right section. The shelves are inspiring. The book ladders are whimsical, yet practical. The smell of old books makes her happy. Spectra loses focus.

She snaps back. She's no closer to understanding how to lift the fog.

I should ask the librarian, she thinks.

This is a big step for Spectra because she likes to do things by herself. It's rare for her to seek help when she goes on adventures. In fact, she thinks seeking help ruins the fun most of the time. She likens it to playing a video game with a game genie or cheat codes or a guidebook. The fun of adventure is in the discovery.

Spectra spots a help desk. She finds an older woman behind a counter. The woman has unkempt grey hair. It's long and wavy. The woman is wearing oversize glasses with decorative frames. She's taking notes on a scratchpad as Spectra walks up to the counter.

"Are you the librarian?"

"Does Roy Rogers issue a trigger warning when he rides into town?"

"Ummm…" Spectra says in confusion.

"Is it the desk? The glasses? The nametag? It was the glasses, wasn't it!" The woman winks and adjusts her frames.

After an awkward silence Spectra asks, "Could you please help me find a book about fog, Miss?"

Suddenly the librarian became serious. She glances past Spectra and surveys the rest of the library. Her voice lowers to a whisper.

"Don't recklessly huck that word around in public, Dearie," the librarian says.

Spectra tenses up in her spine.

The librarian continues, "Go to the small study room in the back and I'll meet you there."

The quiet environment of a library is normally relaxing. It allows for thinking without distraction. Spectra, momentarily, isn't sure she likes the quiet. The hushed words from the librarian continue to tickle her neck.

Spectra finds the small study room in the back of the library. There's a wooden desk and four padded chairs. The green chalk board is filled with calculus. It must have been a long study session because the chalk equations blend into the white clouds that they're replacing.

She feels an uncomfortable silence as she sits down. It reminds her of waiting in the principal's office. The canvas chair pad isn't helping Spectra sit still.

The librarian scurries in and frantically shuts the door behind her. She inadvertently towers over Spectra, forgetting to sit down and relax. *Thunk.* The librarian sets down a large leather-bound book with gold-leafed edges.

Across the front of the book in embossed script reads, "*The Smoke of the Sinister.*"

The librarian licks her long middle finger and sets it firmly along the top right corner of the pages as she deliberately scans through to find one specific section.

"Mmmhmm. Yes. Ah. No, no."

The book is at least a thousand pages long and is filled with both text and diagrams.

Spectra becomes nervous. *What did the cover say, again?* She speaks up with a shy voice, "I'm not sure this is the right book for me, Miss. 'Sinister' sounds—"

"Shhhh, chiiild."

Spectra slinks back in her chair. Her fingers are glistening with sweat even as they grow cold. Each turn of the page fills her with uneasiness.

"Ahhhahhh…" the librarian says. "This is the section I'm looking for." Her outstretched index finger steadies down on a chapter entitled, "The Magic Sled of Nir."

"Look up to find the Magic Sled of Nir," reads the

librarian. "There is a path through Fourier Woods to a gate. The path bifurcates and stretches in two directions: toward Refarm and toward Fomacula. Should the rider of the Magic Sled of Nir travel through the Gate of Splitsies, she shall be split in two."

Spectra doesn't like the sound of that.

"One shall walk down each path, differing only in what they each encounter. Each one whole, each one identical."

That's not as bad as being cut in half, Spectra thinks.

"Should one seek recombination, she must travel through the Couplera Gate with the Magic Sled of Nir."

A second gate?

"The origin of the smoke of the sinister differs from the smooth dexter."

Spectra is becoming confused. She tries not to hurt herself in the confusion.

"Refarm compares favorably with Fomacula. These deviations extend beyond the surface. Remove the origin of the smoke to form a clear veneer in the sinister."

"That's how I get rid of the fog?" Spectra asks.

"It appears so. It seems like quite the riddle to me. I don't think I understand it," says the librarian.

"But how am I supposed to complete my quest if I don't even understand what I'm trying to do? And who is Dexter?"

"I don't know, but if I were you, I would start with the first step. It looks like you need the Magic Sled of Nir."

"Where is that?" Spectra asks.

"I don't know that either, but I wish you the best of luck, child."

4

The librarian returns to work but leaves the book.

Spectra knows the riddle said she could look up the location. She rereads through the chapter on the Magic Sled of Nir to see if she missed where it is stored. It's not in that chapter so she flips rapidly through the text. She finds nothing on the first pass. There's a glossary, but it only points right back to the same chapter.

Could the riddle be that I must take this book with me?

Spectra closes the cover and picks it up to examine it. She turns it over and then back. She lightly bounces it in the air to check the weight. It's too heavy to carry all day. She opens the book up once again and flips back to the section about the sled. There's information about paths and a gate, but no directions. She gives up in frustration.

Spectra takes the book back to the librarian and hands it to her. "Thank you," she says.

"No problem," the librarian says. "If there's anything I can do to help within the confines of the library, please let me know."

"Thank you," Spectra says again.

"You have my support, child. Even if I can't go with you."

"I don't know where to find the sled," Spectra says. "Do you?"

"It was just as much of a riddle to me as it was to you. I'm sorry child. You will have to figure that out by yourself."

Spectra's shoulders sink.

Unsure, but not subdued, she leaves the library, directionless again.

Ivv is sullen in the haze. People are gloomy. Spectra walks through the central square another time, racking her brain to the Tetris of clues. She notices that even the tree branches appear to be drooping.

If I were a magic sled, where would I be?

There's a grass and concrete amphitheater down the way that could be promising, but it generally doesn't have random stuff in it. There's a community garden that always surprises her, but it seems too well-tended to yield anything unplanned. There's a house built by early settlers in the area on the edge of town. It's in disarray, but there's plenty of junk. None of these seem likely to Spectra.

Some people say that you always find something in the last place you look. It's technically true because you stop looking when you find your sled. It doesn't mean, however, that a sled would be found in the last place that one would expect it to be. That would be ridiculous.

Look up to find the Magic Sled of Nir…

Spectra considers the meaning of the phrase. If it was a riddle, and she decides that it is, then it would be better interpreted differently. Most riddles are clever jokes paired with a mental scavenger hunt. In this case, she takes it to mean that she should literally look above the ground.

Around the village, many buildings had at least two stories. The town hall has two stories. Lots of shops have two stories. There even an old church with a giant steeple near the edge of town.

I bet it's in the steeple of the old church, Spectra thinks.

15

Spectra travels to the old church and is delighted to see that it's empty. It's a beautiful church with large doors and colorful stained glass, but it hasn't had a fresh coat of paint in decades. It isn't flashy, and it isn't large. What it lacks in footprint, it makes up for in its pleasing-sounding old bell.

Spectra opens the front door and peeks in.

She doesn't see movement.

A proper ninja will always assess a situation before she sneaks behind the pews. If a ninja is caught in church, she is compelled to confess.

Past the alter is a back area, reserved for the clergy. There's an unlocked door that leads to a dark and winding staircase made of worn out old stone. From the top of the staircase bleeds just enough sunlight to allow Spectra to climb upstairs without tripping.

A mighty iron bell with a vibrant patina hangs peacefully at the top.

There's no sled.

Spectra is disappointed. She told herself that the adventure wouldn't be easy, but she didn't expect that to mean that it would be hard to figure out. She's not opposed to the difficulty of, say, sneaking into a church, but the riddle seems unfair. She wants clear requirements.

The bell tower acts as a veranda for Spectra. She sets her forearm down on the window sill. She crosses the other arm at the elbow and forms a chinrest.

She likes being up high in the bell tower. It allows her to see out upon the world. She wonders what it would be like to look down from a skyscraper in some big city. *Do the people look like ants?* She figures it must be hard to find compassion for people when they look like ants from a certain point of view.

A slight breeze blows hair a strand of hair from her ponytail in front of her eyes.

Spectra pulls the strand back. As her wrist passes her

field of view, she sees a giant chestnut tree. A scatter spray of nuts lines the grass below it. It's tall enough to fit the riddle and she can't see through the leaves. The sled could be hidden in the chestnut tree.

Right as she is about to pull away from the window sill, she sees somebody running up to the tree. It's a boy.

It's not just any boy.

It's Liam.

5

Spectra ducks for cover.

Her heart roars into overdrive with the torque of a thousand horses.

If Liam sees me, he's sure to tell Mom and Dad. If they know I snuck out, I'll be grounded until all the chocolate in the world is gone.

She races into planning mode. A ninja should always know how to escape.

She is stuck in the tower, but the door to the church faces away from the tree. If she just goes back toward the central square, her brother certainly won't see her. She would have to be quiet, but he's occupied with his own adventure and doesn't have a reason to look back in her direction.

The heartbeat thumping through Spectra's chest eases back to normal.

She army-crawls over to the staircase so as not to be seen through the window. After a couple steps, she is free to stand again. True relaxation comes as she descends back toward ground level. A few steps from the bottom, she stops.

An irritating thought enters her consciousness.

What if the sled is in the tree? I can't let Liam get it first!

There's a concept called in economics called a Stackelberg game used to describe naturally occurring situations. A leader makes a move and a follower reacts accordingly. It's sometimes seen in poker as an aggressive bet or in the stock market as a violent move in either direction which causes others to change their strategy. The most illustrative example of where this concept arises is in prison escape. A guard's known route around the grounds forces a would-be escapee to flee in an opportune time and location. Escapees plan their escape around the prison guard. The prison knows that's what an escapee would do. Both sides act accordingly. Nash equilibrium is reached when both parties know the strategies the other could take, such as when a prison knows that shift changes are strategically vulnerable.

Liam doesn't realize that he is in a Stackelberg game. He did, however, hear about a treasure in or around the tree from his friend Mason. Now he is on the lookout for anybody that might steal the treasure from him. He is acting as if he does know that he's in a Stackelberg game.

Liam's going to climb the chestnut tree before Spectra can. As the follower, Spectra must somehow make a move that allows her to get the opportunity to climb the tree first. A Stackelberg game is extremely difficult for a follower to win. That's why ninjas love Stackelberg games. It's also why it's Spectra's favorite type of game. She recites a poem that she wrote:

Around the corner, up and down the same
He repeats a path, which seems super lame
Sneaking around him is the ninja's aim
In the undetected Stackelberg game

Spectra weighs her options from the safety of the old church.

Liam is walking at the base of the tree. He is deciding

which branches to climb. His path could be erratic. He could start climbing at any moment. She must distract Liam as he walks around the base of the tree. If he suspects somebody is trying to distract him, he will assume Mason or Raymond is pulling a prank on him. They always do that. If he thinks there's a prank, it will make him jump up into the tree in panic. He must be distracted, and Spectra must make him think it isn't one of his friends pulling a prank.

It would be an absolute tragedy if Liam got the sled. Spectra's whole day would be ruined.

A sailor's knot forms in her gut.

Spectra glances around. She looks at the stained-glass windows. They are translucent, but not transparent. Light can get through, by a person can't just see through it very easily. It's like the fog, only much prettier and more colorful.

There's a sound of bark scraping off the trunk of the tree.

Spectra's toes curl in her boots. Her eyes widen.

She must act fast.

In a split-second of haste, she comes up with a plan. She rushes back up the staircase to the top of the bell tower, circling the staircase with a hand on the wall. She grabs the rope and rings the bell. Twice. A third time.

Her ears physically hurt from the sound. She cringes into a ball on the ground.

Spectra pauses and tries to listen for Liam, although she isn't sure that she can hear anything after the deafening bell.

The sound of bark scraping off the tree has stopped and been replaced by ringing. Liam must suspect that it's the top of the hour, Spectra figures. He's not climbing. He must not think that one of his friends is pulling a prank.

Knowing she must act quickly, she rises back to her feet.

Spectra rounds her way back down the staircase. No sounds from outside make it to the staircase and she is a thoughtful ninja that knows the reverse must also be true. The smooth steps make little more than sound of a barely audible tap of a finger on a slate façade.

Spectra reaches the bottom of the staircase.

She pitters past the pews, down the aisle, and to the front doors.

She turns the cold handle and gently opens to the world. The air from outside rushes in first and catches her off guard as the morning light streams past a ball of hair.

"Spectra!" shouts Liam.

6

Magic tricks, not the real kind like in Harry Potter, but the fake kind with a magician, rely on sleight of hand. These tricky fake magicians, which aren't wizards and don't even have wands, mind you, misdirect an audience with something shiny in their left hand while they have a cute and fluffy bunny in their right. This works for two reasons. First, the audience don't realize there's a fluffball munching on tasty lettuce in his right hand, so they don't search for the adorable pink rabbit ears. And second, they didn't go to Hogwarts either, so they don't realize that the magician is distracting them with the shiny object. He pushes it far away from the cute little scrunching nose of a silent bunny and the audience never knows why.

Spectra was the bunny in this situation. She tried to make the bell her shiny object. The problem – the part she didn't think through – is that there is only one door leading to both the bunny and the bell. That is quite the mistake. Spectra is a ninja, but she's not a magician. At least not the fake kind. Despite already being thirteen, she is still holding out hope that an owl from Hogwarts might come and tell her she's a wizard. In any case, her plan was not good.

Liam shouts Spectra's name and it spikes right through her forehead and rings around like a penny in a vortex. Her calves tense up. They release when her knees hyperextend.

"Are you okay? You look flabbergasted," Liam says.

"Just flummoxed," Spectra replies.

Sometimes when Spectra is trying to be clever, she is little more than an ouroboros. Those are the snakes that bite their own tail. This was clearly one of those times.

"What are you doing out here, sis?" Liam asks. "You are supposed to be in your room, grounded. Did Mom and Dad let you out?"

Liam innocently stares straight into Spectra's eyes when he asks the question. His voice echoes in the vaulted ceilings of the church. He's both curious and a little vexed. The situation still hasn't registered in his mind, but it registers clearly upon his face.

"First off, please don't tell Mom and Dad. This fog is making them crazy. I don't want to still be grounded when you get your first job. Second off, I'm searching for something. It's very important."

"Me too!" says Liam. "Mason said there was a treasure out by the tree. Or in the tree. I think he might have said in the tree, but I'm not sure."

Sometimes Liam struggles with details.

"I'm not looking for a treasure," Spectra says, "but if I find it, I'll give you some."

"You can't just go look for *my* treasure without *me*!" Liam objects.

Liam's tone comes off as more defensive than Spectra was hoping for. Spectra knows that the plan must change.

"Let's make a deal," she says. "I'll help you look for your treasure in the chestnut tree, but if I find what I'm looking for, I get to keep it. And in return, you don't tell Mom and Dad anything."

Liam thinks about the deal for a second. He looks up

to his big sister and is too trusting of her. She rarely outright lies to him, but there are times when a little deception and misdirection is necessary in a sibling rivalry. He's easily deceived, in part, because he craves the opportunity to spend more time with her. The lonelier he feels, the more gullible he becomes.

"Oh boy, yeah," Liam says with enthusiasm.

Spectra doesn't tell Liam that she's looking for a magic sled. Liam is too focused on the non-existent treasure to ask. It's a sly move. She doesn't want to excite him and get stuck with him all day. It's selfish, she knows, but this is *her* mission and she is determined to complete it *by herself*.

Liam glows with excitement and stands taller.

A big sister naturally doesn't want to share things with her little brother. She wants to have her own things and not have to play with the stupid little kid toys all the time. The little brother, in turn, looks at the waaaay better big kid toys that his super-smart big sister gets to play with, and wants nothing more than to play with her.

It's a one-way dynamic.

That also means it's exploitative.

She could use it to her advantage.

Spectra also prides herself on being compassionate, which, to her own chagrin, compels her to empathize with Liam and let him tag along far too often. This is the opposite of exploiting her advantage, but it also makes her a pretty good big sister.

This type of situation is irreconcilable for such an important adventure, but that doesn't really matter in the context in which Spectra finds herself. Spectra is a ninja and her most important goal is to not get caught. She did sneak out of the house and she knows that she needs Liam to remain an ally for the day. An ally at arms-length, but an ally nonetheless.

She doesn't care two hoots about the fake treasure that Liam's dumb friend, Mason, made up, but she knows that

Liam cares about the treasure, so Spectra must pretend to care.

There's a tight line to be walked.

Be sly, Spectra thinks.

Spectra Morris places her hand on Liam's shoulder blade. She joins forces with her brother.

7

There are thirteen thousand four hundred eighty-five chestnuts under the large tree and nine thousand and one of them are still cloaked in a spiky green armor. If you add in the twigs and pointy rocks, there are fifteen thousand and four ground-dwelling foot barbs waiting patiently to cause serious pain. It's worse than the spilled-over bucket of Liam's Legos.

A wide band of ducks migrate overhead in a linear array. The mallards can be heard, but they hide from view with the thick cover of fog.

Spectra feels dread over the possibility of falling from a branch onto such a precarious ground. She takes the selfish route. She decides that Liam should be the tree-climber.

The sturdy tree has a trunk far too large for Liam to reach his arms around, so he'll need help to get up to the lowest branch.

"Come on," Spectra says. "I'll give you a lift."

Liam is pleased that he gets to do the climbing.

Spectra interlaces her fingers and forms a sling for Liam to step on. His foot feels heavier than she expects. *Has he gained five pounds in the last few months?* Liam reaches up and grabs the lowest branch. He pulls himself up and swings his left leg onto the tree. From there, he's able to shimmy and roll into a straddle.

"What do you see up there?" Spectra asks.

Liam climbs higher and higher. The fog covers his movements. Little bits of bark float down and land in Spectra's eyes as she attempts to watch in anxiety. Chestnuts start to drop. Spectra narrowly avoids getting hit in the face with her quick ninja reflexes.

"I don't see it," Liam yells down.

"*What* don't you see?"

"The treasure. I don't see the treasure."

"But do you see anything else up there?"

Spectra is still trying to keep her secret. She doesn't want Liam to know she is looking for a magic sled. He loves magic.

"Like what? Spikeballs?" asks Liam.

"Something hand-crafted or made by a person."

"Tell me what I'm looking for, Spectra!"

She pauses. Is it worth it to tell him? What harm could it do? The little brat is helping her, so maybe it's the least she could do. She settles on a half-truth.

"It's a sled, Liam. I misplaced a sled."

There's an uncomfortable silence. *Is he looking for the sled? Did he find it?*

Spectra takes a half step backward. She wonders if she made a mistake.

Liam starts laughing uncontrollably. "That's ridiculous!" he says. "You put a sled in the top of a tree? How? You can't even get up here by yourself! How would you carry a sled with you?"

Spectra sinks. *Oh no.*

Telling Liam was a mistake, but not in the way that Spectra feared.

She recomposes herself. "Just forget it, Liam." She says. "I knew it wasn't up there. Just being careful, you know?"

Liam continues to giggle.

Spectra feels like she is losing control. She impulsively attacks. "You didn't think there was going to be a treasure up there, did you?"

"At least I don't think I put it here," he retorts with a chuckle.

Fluffmallow! He may be young and dumb, but the kid can be smart sometimes.

"Just come on down, Liam. There's nothing up there."

Liam is still laughing too hard to start climbing down. There's a scraping sound. Some chestnuts fall. Liam grabs on tight to keep from chasing them to the ground.

Spectra loses sympathy and backs away from the tree trunk. She's fed up with her brother and his petulant laugh. She finds an empty patch of grass and sits down, facing away from the tree.

The fog blocks her view back into Ivv.

Liam starts climbing down.

Spectra runs her hand over the dew. She readjusts her skirt.

Liam gets down to the lowest branch and asks Spectra for help with getting down to the ground.

Spectra pulls some blades of grass. She doesn't want to help. The plan has been a disaster and now her brother, the one laughing at her, is asking for her help. She isn't in the mood and decides to be reticent.

"Please," Liam says.

"Not right now," Spectra responds with slightly more animosity than she intends.

Liam is off-put, but he can't stay in the tree.

Spectra lets her mind wander. She thinks about other places to look for the Magic Sled of Nir.

Liam swings down from sitting on a branch to a hang. The skin on his wrists and palms get torn up. He drops down and lands on a chestnut with his left heel, which rolls his ankle, buckling his knee, and landing him squarely on his butt. He gets impaled by three very lucky spikeballs.

There's a yell that can be heard two villages over.

"Ow!!!"

Spectra jerks her head like a finch. She sees her brother on the ground. A rush of adrenaline hits her fingers and toes. In a blur, she rushes over to him. *I caused this*, she thinks to herself. *It was my fault. I should have helped him.*

Liam's face is fragile. He pulls the chestnuts from his butt and throws them at the ground in frustration. He's clearly in pain, but he's not the kind of boy that lets tears reach the outside world. He turns a glaring face at Spectra, one that she will never forget. He doesn't have to say anything.

Spectra's tongue hugs the roof of her mouth. Her cheeks slump past her lips. She knows she messed up. She breaks into fifteen thousand and four pieces inside. Every one of them is guilt-ridden and ashamed.

8

Spectra embraces Liam in her arms. She tries to hold him tight and let him know that she's there for him. Tears form, but she holds them back with all her will.

Liam isn't having it.

As Spectra tries to mend the gap between them, Liam pushes her away.

"It'll be alright," she says.

"No, Spectra. It won't."

"Do you need to go to the doctor?"

He may only be nine, but he's already trying to act tough. "My butt is made of hardened alloy," he says. "It's the chestnuts that need a doctor!"

Spectra breaks her seriousness in a smirk.

"What can I do for you?" she asks.

"You should have just stayed in your room where you were grounded," he says with some fervor. "You're making things worse. If you wanted to help, the time was when I was in the tree."

"I'm sorry, Liam. I really am."

"You should go be sorry by yourself somewhere. Go play with your dumb sled."

Spectra is filled with a second dose of worry. Now she

worries that she has done irreparable harm to the relationship with her little brother. She worries that he will turn bitter and cut her off and then she'll have nobody she can scheme with.

Then she is hit with another worry.

What if Liam tells Mom and Dad?

In a regatta, sailboats race to a buoy and back. In one direction they go downwind and get to open their spinnakers, which are like parachutes. This is where the phrase 'wind at your back' comes from. It's the relaxing part of a regatta. Sailing upwind is more difficult. A captain must tack back and forth in a zigzag pattern. The lead boat tacks first and the others must be on the ready to tack so that they don't run into the leader. When Spectra was the follower in her Stackelberg game, she was sailing upwind and she successfully tacked to avoid crashing. Then, when Liam was in the tree, she rounded the buoy and hoisted the spinnaker. It might have been smooth sailing from there, but Spectra had a breeze saturate her spinnaker, broaching, and causing roll. Her rudder surfaced. When something like that happens, if the mainsail sheet isn't eased, the boom is going to go for a swim. Spectra was broaching. She eased the mainsail sheet.

"It's a magic sled," she says.

Liam's animosity is met with confusion.

"Yeah right!"

"No really, it is. I read it in a book."

"And I read about magic wizards," Liam says. "It doesn't mean they exist."

Spectra is a little more hurt by this than she should be. On the one hand, she knows that Harry Potter isn't real. Hogwarts doesn't exist. But on the other hand, what if it does. It probably doesn't. But if there's a slim chance it does, she's ready for wizarding school.

"This was a non-fiction book. That means everything in it is true," Spectra says about *The Smoke of the Sinister*, while still thinking that the Harry Potter books might also be non-fiction.

"What did it say about the magic sled, exactly?" Liam asks.

"Well, it was sort of a riddle," she says with a struggle. "It's called The Magic Sled of Nir. The book says you can ride it through the Gate of Splitsies to remove this fog."

As the words leave her mouth, she has a slight hesitation and dread of gullibility. It was quite a lot to take in and repeating it made it sound a little ridiculous.

Liam blinks in thought.

"Where's Nir?"

Spectra is taken aback by the question.

"Ummm. I'm not sure," she murmurs. "But it didn't say the sled was *in* Nir. It just said that's where it's from."

"Wait. You're looking for a sled – a *magic* sled – in Ivv, when a book said that it was from Nir?"

The fear of being duped grows in Spectra's stomach.

She becomes defensive. She realizes she needs Liam to come with her so that he doesn't tell their parents that she snuck out of the house.

"There *is* a magic sled and I'm going to find it, Liam. You can come if you'd like to help me. And anyway, you're already looking for a fake treasure that stupid Mason made up."

"He didn't make it up and he isn't stupid."

"Yes, he did, and you should join me."

"No," he replies in defiance.

Earlier in the summer, before the fog had moved in, there was a beautiful June day without a cloud in the sky. Ruby and Hugh brought Spectra and Liam out to a minor league baseball game. The whole family had those hotdogs that stick out past the bun. Spectra was only 12 at the time. She and Liam were partners in crime that day.

During the middle of the sixth inning, Spectra was starting to get hungry again. She turned from her seat and saw fans milling around with ice cream on the concourse. With a tap on the forearm and a bob of her head, she got Liam to notice the ice cream too. Spectra and Liam love ice cream. They love it almost as much as cookies.

Spectra asked Hugh for a couple dollars and gave him the puppy dog eyes. Hugh gave her a ten and Ruby said, "get some for your brother too."

The ice cream stand had four flavors.

Spectra sampled each flavor, one-by-one, licking the creamy treat off the sample spoons. Liam knew the rub. They were working together. He was sampling each flavor in a *different* order. When they finished sampling all four, they asked for a fifth sample.

The scooper guy had a hunch that they had tried all the flavors before. He said something about it. Spectra said that she hadn't tried the cookie dough flavor yet, that was her brother. Liam said that he hadn't tried the chocolate with chocolate chunks, that was his sister. The scooper guy was none the wiser. They got their fifth sample scoop. Then they ordered a scoop each. It was the perfect ninjaing cooperation caper.

So, Spectra wasn't fundamentally opposed to working with her brother. They worked quite well together.

She just hadn't wanted to work with him on saving the world from the oppressive fog.

But when Liam rejected her offer, Spectra was devastated.

9

Liam gives a good long look. He narrows his eyes, furrows his brows, and purses his lips before turning and walking away.

Spectra is left all alone again.

She had thought she wanted to be alone, but it feels empty now.

"Liam!" she shouts.

He stops but doesn't turn. His right heel is left dramatically off the ground. Spectra knows he is making a show of having been stopped.

"Please don't tell Mom and Dad on me. I'm really sorry."

He starts walking again. The fog puts distance between them quicker than expected as he fades away from sight.

"I'll get you some ice cream to make up for it!"

It's a last-ditch effort, but bribery can work on a little brother.

Liam doesn't slow to listen to her plea.

Spectra wonders if he hears it. She knows that he does.

Spectra slouches and starts walking back toward town.
Is he right? How could it even be possible that the Magic Sled of

Nir is in Ivv? Wouldn't that make it the Magic Sled of Ivv?

Her questions sink her morale.

The hill slanting back into town produces heavy steps and an exaggerated gait from Spectra's boots. The grass is patchy and uneven. Her outsoles struggle to grip the moist blades. Her arms slink past her sides.

There are more questions running through Spectra's head and more uncertainty in her plan than when she started. *Was this a mistake?*

Spectra has always seen herself as more of a ninja than a wizard. If she was a wizard, she would be a wizard without a magic sled. She doesn't even have a wand. And she's still waiting on that owl. If she's a ninja, then she isn't a very sly one. She feels lost. Whatever she is, she wants to be a great one.

Spectra decides that she's a ninja and she can't keep a bummer attitude. *Who has ever heard of a mopey ninja?* She takes Taylor Swift's advice and literally starts shaking her body. It has a magical way of working.

Despite picking up her demeanor, she still needs to pick up a plan.

As she enters town, there's an apothecary on her left and haberdashery flanking her right. Neither seems likely to house a magic sled. She turns down Izatt Street and heads to the sporting goods store on E. Buck Lane.

She finds expensive exercise equipment and signature baseball mitts at the sporting goods store. It seems too big to be as empty of shoppers as it is. There's a section for bikes, but nothing for sledding. There are multiple racks of t-shirts.

Spectra finds a clerk.

"Hi sir," she says. "Do you happen to have any sleds?"

"Whatchu need a sled for?" he says in an aggressive tone.

Adults who use an aggressive tone toward kids can easily frighten them. Spectra is used to angry adults, after a month of fog-induced crankiness. She has a meanness shield.

"I'm on an important mission," she says. "An adventure."

"Well, you'd have to traverse a long way to find any snow this time of year."

"I'm willing to try," she responds with spunk.

"No, we don't have any sleds, and if that's what you need, your little adventure is going to be a little bit littler than you think it is."

Spectra is more disappointed in the cranky pants than anything else. She's exhausted from all the negativity. Sled or no sled, she must find a way to push the smoke out of her village.

"Thank you, sir," she says, politely.

Spectra leaves the sporting goods store, once again, empty-handed.

Without having a plan, Spectra instinctively starts walking back toward the Fujimoto Library. That's where she first learned about the sled and there's a gravitational pull to be back in control, with some knowledge at least.

She approaches the building and halts to get a good look at it.

Professor Tina Seelig of Stanford says to look at terrible ideas through the lens of possibility. She says that some of the best ideas, some of the most creative ones, are found by taking the dumbest ones you can think of and trying to figure out how to make them work. She says that it's one of the ways that somebody like Spectra can make her own luck.

Look up to find the Magic Sled of Nir, she thinks.

The library is worn and made of stucco, but in that way, it looks like a good book that has been checked out an appropriate number of times. Spectra inhales to find out if it smells like the tattered pages of thrilling fantasy novel too.

What would be a dumb place to put a sled? she thinks.

It's a riddle. Spectra has read quite a few adventure books. Those are her favorite kind. If this were an adventure book, the riddle, she decides, wouldn't be saying to look the sled up in the text. No, if she were a hero on a journey, the riddle would mean the sled is—

Spectra's eyes light up. She lets out an audible gasp.

10

The village of Ivv is small, but they are incorporated, so they think they aren't that small. There are smaller communities nearby that aren't incorporated, so Ivv feels proud of itself. The old church isn't as popular as it used to be. There's a new church in town with a pristine white steeple—one without a bell—that caused quite the village-wide argument when it was erected. Small towns are like that—they don't know how to handle change. Big cities are always tearing down, building up, and reinventing themselves in a cutthroat tale of evolution and taxes, but the small town is content just to be as it is. Even the smallest changes turn heads in Ivv. A flipped-up mailbox flag gets noticed. When the local school repainted its sign, the topic of conversation hovered on it for a week.

The restaurants in Ivv don't have fancy floors and tables, they just have, floors and tables. They aren't something special worth mentioning. Walls have decorations, but not design. Kitschy local memorabilia rests above every booth. Villagers are okay with things just being what they are, not needing to them to be statement pieces. It's why they see folks in the big cities as pretentious.

The definition of a place is different in Ivv. There's a pile of rocks and it's a place. The stop sign is a place. People say, "go to the stop sign, turn left, and you can't miss it. If you see the pile of rocks, you've gone too far." The types of plants in the planter boxes become as useful as street names when giving directions. Most of the streets don't have sidewalks.

There aren't theme parks or art galleries. There's a collection of rusted old cars parked on the grass at one of the older houses on the edge of town. That counts as art simply because it is different. People in Ivv wouldn't know what to do with an art gallery. There are no days off for the adults in Ivv. Days are long, weeks are short, years are long, and lives are short. It's the opposite of a city at all four intervals.

A big city ebbs and flows, like a beating heart, with rush hour, at a steady year-round pace. The village of Ivv is more like a Jack-in-the-Box, laying low, only to pop up in full force when the time is right. The number of people in Ivv quadruples on the weekends in October, when the fields turn into hay mazes. Cities never quadruple, but they always change.

Living in a small town, the rapid change in a big city is unfathomable to Spectra. The colorful LED lights, the skyscrapers, and flavors from regions of the world a small-town girl only knows from a map form a surreal quality. That's why it's so easy to believe in magic in a small town. So many things are out there that don't exist in Ivv, so why wouldn't a magic sled also be out there?

Spectra believes in the Magic Sled of Nir because she believes in Belgium. She hasn't been to Belgium, but she's read about it. They have waffles. She believes in the Magic Sled of Nir because her neighbors went to the big city and came back with a vacuum robot that picks up dust all by itself. It's hard to know what's real and what isn't at her age. So, she takes the position that a magical world exists, if only she has the determination to find it.

Books fill her imagination with the magical. There are books in the library on everything from tug boats to the space station. She's never seen either of those. There are books with the math that proves that steam engines are possible. Spectra deeply loves math because she sees it as a magic wand. The library, to her, is the greatest tool a wizard can have. From there, all things are possible. She sees even the magical things that could never exist. To her, the library can make it so.

Later that day, when it gets dark, the October crowds from the city will flow into Ivv. Hugh and Ruby plan to hide inside, away from the hay maze. Liam has been begging to go. It's a haunted maze that's targeted towards teenagers and Liam isn't quite old enough. To him, that makes it the most desirable type of place.

Liam is a fan of bad horror and sci-fi movies. He had a sleepover the previous weekend to watch a Sharknado marathon with his friends from school. They stayed up until 2 am and made sleeping bag forts. When they finally fell asleep, Mason tried to get Liam to pee his pants by placing Liam's hand in water. Raymond led them to make prank calls and go play ding, dong, ditch.

Ivv is a wonderful place in October, and truthfully, Hugh would admit, the fog helps make October feel right. Ruby still doesn't like it. She can't get past the nasty HOA and PTA meetings.

There are crunchy-looking leaves on the ground all around Ivv. Liam loves to stomp on them as he walks down the street. Spectra doesn't like the leaves anymore, after Hugh made her rake the yard two weeks ago. She still likes Halloween, however. She is excited to dress up as Hermione Granger.

The library will get dressed up for Halloween too, but not for another week. They stream spiderwebs and have a big pumpkin carving party for the kids in town. They put a skeleton on display and label all the bones. There is even a room where they install black lights. To a kid, not many things are more magical than black lights.

Spectra looks up at the library and believes in the Magic Sled of Nir again. Not only that, she believes that *The Smoke of the Sinister* is a magic book, and so it, too, has tricks of its own. She figures that it already knows more about the world than she does. Maybe the book knows more than just the past too. Maybe it knows where the magic sled is.

11

There's an abandoned house on the edge of Ivv. There isn't a fence around the yard and Spectra is able to search among the piles of junk that she finds there. Thankfully, she's up-to-date on all her vaccinations, including the tetanus shot.

No neighbors can see her through the fog.

No missing items would be noticed.

Beyond the rusted jalopy and past the completely unnecessary broken school bus, Spectra finds scrap metal and wood.

Why keep all this junk?

Spectra is careful around the metal scraps. Some of the pieces look incredibly sharp. If she gets a cut, she'll get caught by her parents. It's not a danger she would have faced in her room if she had stayed there all day. A cut would make it obvious that she snuck out.

Out of the corner of her eye, she spots what she was looking for.

Spectra slowly climbs over the loose shrapnel, placing each step firmly onto grass, where available. In places without visible ground, she finds large, heavy objects where she softly tests the balance with her toes.

She reaches a long two-by-four. She removes it from underneath an old red wagon. The beam is even longer than she thought. *It's perfect!* It's exactly what she was looking for, other than the partially extruding nails.

She picks up the long wooden two-by-four. It's heavy. *This might be too much weight for me*, she thinks.

Spectra decides to carry the plank by herself anyway.

On the back side of the library is a pile of loose rocks. That's where she is taking the two-by-four. It's only a couple blocks, but it might as well be a couple miles. As she carries the large piece of wood, she stops after thirty-seven steps. She lets it drop. Her arms are exhausted.

Spectra catches her breath and then decides that she can drag one end of the wood behind her along the ground. Using this tactic makes the two-by-four feel about half as heavy. The grass is uneven and bounces the plank in several directions. The heft of the wood pushes Spectra into a wobble, but she makes progress.

After lugging the wood off the grass, she is faced with a gravel road. It makes noise. Pebbles jump off the ground as she drags the two-by-four.

Spectra looks around to see if anybody is within earshot.

She decides that she's alone.

After much effort, Spectra makes it to the giant pile of loose rocks. She drops the two-by-four and collapses in exhaustion.

Spectra regains her composure.

It takes all the strength she can muster, but she's able to pick the beam up into a vertical orientation. She walks it up the pile.

With a mighty wind-up, Spectra lifts the two-by-four into the air and then uses all her muscles to auger it straight into the rocks. It penetrates by almost a full foot. The pebbles underneath her feet slip. Spectra loses her balance. She hits the pile of rocks with a loud crash.

When Spectra realizes what has happened, it's too late. Her knees and elbows are busted up and bloody. She starts to worry. Her parents will surely know she snuck out.

Spectra assesses the damage. She is bleeding, but it isn't a gushing blood. She doesn't need to go to the hospital. There are bruises up and down her legs, but nothing is broken. There's some debris and dust that's easy to wipe off. The rocks below her have settled. She decides that she can tough it out and continue. Getting scuffed up is never pleasant and never a goal, but it isn't the first time she discovered some red marks in the pursuit of adventure.

The two-by-four is still standing tall at the top of the pile of rocks. It looks like a flagpole claiming a mountain.

Spectra climbs back up the pile to the two-by-four. She pushes it from the top so that it leans toward the library. The rocks underneath her feet continue to shift, but Spectra maintains a steady boot to prop herself safely up. She keeps pushing the two-by-four until it touches down on the library wall. It forms a bridge for her to climb onto the roof.

With both hands, she bear-crawls her way up the two-by-four from the pile of rocks onto the roof. Her hands struggle with the grip, but she keeps her balance firmly centered. Looking down makes her anxious, but she must do so to continue.

She climbs all the way past the roofline until her legs can hang down to meet it. This is becoming a habit. Twice already today has she walked on a roof. She really must be a ninja.

Her boots set flat and she stands up straight. She exhales and then starts breathing heavily to refill her suffocating arteries. It turns out that it was more nerve-wracking than she had realized.

She gazes around the rooftop.

There, on the other side of the roof, was a black object

that she can't quite make out. She runs to it. Spectra is overcome with joy and relief when the object turns out to be a sled. She knows that it has to be the Magic Sled of Nir.

12

There's a slight breeze on the roof. Wind is often stronger above the ground.

Spectra is proud of her accomplishment and she decides that it's okay to take a morning break. She wants to take it all in. She sets up the sled near the edge of the roof and sits on it. From her bag, she pulls out the yogurt and is happy to find that it's still relatively cool. She uses the foil top as a spoon as she savors each bite.

There on a perch above all that is known
She surveys the domain of her time
Passing through mist, she sees only the shown
Deep in the midst of her prime

It feels good to relax after the stress of her morning.

She realizes that she has only just begun her adventure, but already she has achieved something great. Appreciation of accomplishment derives from deliberate contemplation.

Spectra thinks it was quite lucky that she was able to find her way to the Magic Sled of Nir. When she set out just a few hours ago, she didn't even know about the sled. She contemplates the meaning and scale of luck.

There are three kinds of luck. There's an intrinsic luck. Eli Manning was born into a football family with athletic genes. He had intrinsic luck. The second kind of luck is extrinsic luck. When the New England Patriots selected Tom Brady as the 199th pick in the sixth round of the 2000 NFL Draft, that was extrinsic luck. It wasn't obvious that Brady would ever even play in the league at that point. The third kind of luck is instantaneous luck. When Eli Manning passed to David Tyree in Super Bowl XLII and Tyree caught the ball against his helmet, that was instantaneous luck. It was the crucial play that allowed the Giants to beat Tom Brady's undefeated Patriots. There's a hierarchy to luck that is illustrated in that play. The shorter the luck permanence, the more important it is to the outcome of an event.

Spectra decides that her luck on the day has been instantaneous luck.

The cherry yogurt tastes good. The smooth texture allows her to collect her thoughts even more. It isn't ice cream, but it does the trick. The fog prevents her from seeing her neighbors on the ground below, but she knows they are still walking around, troubled as ever. Removing the fog should help all her neighbors, although Spectra is the most concerned about lifting the mood of her parents.

Spectra understands that her adventure is only at the beginning. The Magic Sled of Nir is only a tool that she must use to remove the fog.

The Nobel Prize-winning economist Richard Thaler has a rule that he calls Roth's rule, named after Alvin E. Roth. It states that in equilibrium, it's impossible for you to be happier than your spouse. Put another way, if they're not happy, you're not happy. The couple is collectively only as happy as the least happy partner. *Maybe this extends to an entire village*, Spectra thinks. Or maybe it would if all the villagers cared deeply about each other. It could prove to be empirical evidence for the need of compassion in a village experiencing suffering. And although the fog is affecting all the residents of Ivv, it appears to Spectra that it is not enough to only remove the suffering of one person at a time. A person could be cured, but if they are an empathetic person, upon reaching happiness and being in the company of their neighbors, they would once again return to anguish. Encounters with the rest of the village would bring them back down. She figures that the whole village must be cured all at once. It takes a child to raise a village.

Spectra finishes her yogurt. She cleans up and puts the container back into her backpack. Littering is never acceptable. It makes her feel good to pack out her trash.

She glances down. Her bloody legs are visible past her pleated red skirt. The damage is obvious, but it isn't *terrible*. Spectra knows that she can continue her adventure, even with the dings and scuffs. *The rugged look is kind of nice*, she thinks.

After further reasoning, she also decides that she can cover he arms and legs with a cardigan and jeans when she gets back to her room. *Maybe Mom and Dad won't notice*.

Spectra feels ready to continue with her adventure. She rises to her feet, puts her backpack on, and grabs the sled.

She can't see Fourier Woods, but she knows that's her next destination.

It's time to find the Gate of Splitsies.

13

Getting the sled down off the roof isn't the easiest thing to figure out. It's big and bulky and Spectra needs both hands. She decides to set the sled on the two-by-four and let it slide down to the pile of rocks as if the two-by-four was a zipline. It works surprisingly well.

Spectra decides to climb down feet first, once again in a bear crawl. She has to look between her legs as she steps. It's a slow process, but she's okay taking it as slowly as she needs to in order to remain safe. It's a form a personal responsibility, which she embraces.

She makes it down safely.

Relief overcomes her.

Both going up and down the two-by-four turns out to have been more stressful than she anticipated. She's delighted to be done with it.

Spectra grabs the Magic Sled of Nir and walks down the rock pile onto terra firma.

Fourier Woods is on the other side of Ivv.

Spectra doesn't know how careful she must be as she walks through town with the sled in her hand. *If somebody spots me, they might just think it's weird, but not concerning,* she decides.

The fog helps cloak her movements.

She plays it cool; acts like carrying a sled is completely normal.

Dr. Ophelia, Dr. Thelma, and Dr. Molly are walking by.

"Hello," Spectra says, casually as she passes.

"Well hello Spectra," says Dr. Molly. "Off to go sledding today?"

"You might have to wait until there's some snow," says Dr. Ophelia.

"Oh, this thing," Spectra says, pointing at the sled.

Dr. Thelma acts surprised.

"You know me, always looking for adventure."

"Just don't do anything dangerous," says Dr. Ophelia.

"And if you do, don't get caught," says Dr. Thelma with a wink.

Spectra laughs a little. "Thanks for the concern. I'm not going to do anything dangerous. I'm just off to save the world."

"Another normal Saturday," says Dr. Molly. "Have fun!"

They wave goodbye and then Spectra continues through the village of Ivv.

She manages to make it through the rest of town without getting stopped again. Acting normal and having her 'normal' be 'adventurous' works well.

Patchy natural grass grows in the field prior to entering the woods. There are three green laurels trees jutting out beyond the boundary into the field, welcoming all visitors. The trunks on the laurels twist and writhe as if they had to work to escape the hard soil.

Spectra doesn't know where to find the Gate of Splitsies, but she doesn't want to get lost among the ash, birch, and maple. Becoming disoriented in a place where one can't see twenty feet is one of the most stressful things a hiker can encounter.

Wolf Creek runs through Fourier Woods. Spectra

knows that she can use it to guide her. She traverses along the boundary line with the trees until she finds the running water. There's a trail running parallel. *Follow Wolf Creek and I can't get lost,* she tells herself.

She enters the woods.

It feels quiet. It feels damp. It feels squishy in the mud beneath her boots.

Fourier Woods is an aspirational place. It's true in both senses of the word. It wants to be a great forest. The mountain holly grows thick and hardy, protected by tall and slender mockernut hickory. Fourier Woods is also aspirational in the sense that it is breathing. The maples, the woodpeckers, and even the creek seem to breathe with the energy of life. Walking through Fourier Woods, Spectra feels that it isn't just a place, but a *living* place. The woods are perhaps aspirational to become a great forest in part because the individual parts all breathe in unison, symbiotic in nature.

There's an eerie sensation with the mist. Shrubs rustle. Twigs crack. It's hard to pinpoint the origin of the sounds. Surrounded by trees, the noise dampens, but it also ricochets. It becomes both quieter and starker, but directionless and imprecise.

Spectra's nose grows cold and wet in the woods. Her ears turn red. She becomes more aware of her surroundings. It feels refreshing to be back among the moths and caterpillars. As she proceeds further inward, the mockernut hickory trees take over. They grow mighty. This is their land. Spectra feels small in their presence.

Spectra climbs small knolls and trudges carefully through each ravine. She stays within earshot of Wolf Creek for safety. The water swirls over the riverbed filled with smooth round rocks. It's a beautiful clear creek.

The Smoke of the Sinister mentioned the Gate of Splitsies, but didn't describe what it looks like. Spectra first envisioned a wooden garden gate, perhaps with English Ivy growing on it. Or maybe the wrought iron version of the same thing. She thought it would be something befitting of the nature in which it could be found. Then, as the book described riding the sled through the gate, Spectra's mental image changed.

There's a large gate in Shunde, Foshan, China at the edge of Shunfengshan Park. It's a memorial archway gate, a *Paifeng*. The large arches of white are not only wide enough to ride a sled through, they seem transformational. She could envision that crossing the boundary and passing through a gate like that could be significant. A large gate like that *Paifeng* could have a different place on the other side. The other side wouldn't have to abide by the rules on the side of Ivv. It would not only be a monument, but also a place.

This mental image means that Spectra is looking for a *Moby Dick*, a great white whale of a gate that could be seen from all around. She seeks a leviathan gate of the magnitude necessary to divide two places.

Her expectations aren't met.

She sees colorful blue-beech, white ash, and silverbell trees in red, orange, and yellow, but no canopy piercing gates.

Down the fall-line, she spots something shining through the woods. A glint. The creek is to her left. It flows and meanders, but it isn't a lost creek. It knows where it is going. She follows the stream of water with her eyes through the woods and decides that it isn't the source of the bright reflection. *If the shimmer isn't from water*, she concludes, *it must be the Gate of Splitsies.*

14

The Gate of Splitsies does not meet Spectra's expectations, but she is wowed by the beauty nonetheless. She crests a hill and gets a good look at the structure that sits in the bottom of a dry dell. The gate looks like a fifteen-foot tall silver St. Louis Gateway Arch. It is short enough to hide such that it can only be seen from either side of the dell. Even with the fog cover, it shines through the trees.

This gateway arch, the Gate of Splitsies, is out of place in the woods, but it still feels natural. The dull glint of the polished metal surface is incongruous, but the simple shape and clean lines makes it less dominating and overbearing. Aluminum structures do not naturally grow in the woods, but if they did, maybe they would look like this gate.

Spectra is confronted with two thoughts. First, she realizes that there's no snow and she's supposed to ride the sled. And second, she still isn't sure that she actually wants to be split into two.

She finds a nice flat spot on the top of the hill to set the sled down. It's a black sled that looks wooden but is probably just a veneer. It's less heavy than it seems like it should be. The material is sturdy and firm, nonetheless.

On the bottom are two metal blade runners that extend past the length of the sled. They have an oily coating on them.

Spectra's favorite athlete is Mikaela Shiffrin, the skier. Although the sled is different than skis, Spectra thinks they are analogous in this situation. Shiffrin has incredible focus. She takes ice baths even though they are painfully cold and doesn't go crazy with her fame, like Bode Miller did. Her job as a professional athlete is a serious one and she takes it seriously. Before racing, Shiffrin slips the course, sliding slowly down the hill to get a firm grasp of the topography. Then she closes her eyes and visualizes skiing through the gates before she starts.

Be prepared, Spectra thinks.

She walks down the hill toward the gate. Spectra wants to understand the ground underneath her. She wants to slip the course, just like Mikaela Shiffrin.

There are rocks and leaves and twigs in the detritus. Spectra grabs anything large and throws it out of her way. She wants a clean path down the hill.

Each time a rock hits the ground, a noise echoes through the woods that makes the goal seem all the more real and daring. *That could be the sound of me hitting the dirt*, she thinks. Some rocks hit the neighboring trees. *That could be the sound of my bones breaking*, she thinks. The cold rocks feel hard in her fingers.

When she gets to the gate at the bottom of the dell, she runs her hand over the surface. It's smooth like a countertop and cold to the touch. At the bottom, she finds the following inscription:

Parts Assembled and Spliced on Site
Not Manufactured in Cleveland

That seems weird to Spectra, but so is finding a magic gate in the woods.

She pauses to consider simply walking through.

She doesn't dare.

The Smoke of the Sinister was clear that she would have to ride through the Gate of Splitsies. There are many times when Spectra likes to ignore directions and do her own thing. It's one of her core competencies. She just doesn't think it's wise to ignore directions about being split into two parts.

Spectra closes her eyes again and imagines sliding right through the gate.

When she opens her eyes, she exhales and turns to march back up the hill.

Back at her sled, she is still uncomfortable with the thought of being chopped in half. How would that happen? Would her legs be cut off from her torso? Her left arm cut off from her right? It didn't sound pleasant no matter what.

She considers turning back.

Pride in her adventurous spirit overcomes her. She can handle whatever happens. She didn't come all this way just to chicken out.

Spectra checks the direction of the sled to ensure that it's pointed directly at the center of the gate. She nudges the back of the sled a little bit to the right. There's a slight breeze. She nudges it back a little to the left.

Perfect!

Spectra places her left boot and then her right to either side of the sled, straddling it. She looks over her shoulder as she bends her butt down onto the hard plastic.

Thunk.

Her butt stings from landing on the sled.

She grabs the sides of the sled with her fingers. There's a lip that provides enough grip to feel safe, although Spectra knows she must hold on tight.

She closes her eyes one more time and envisions Mikaela Shiffrin in a starting gate at the top of Beaver

Creek. *Wolf Creek and Beaver Creek are pretty much the same thing*, she assures herself. The vision of Mikaela in her mind starts getting a countdown. Spectra knows that Shiffrin must go by the end of the fifth beep.

Beep.

Spectra starts pushing the sled back to rock herself into a faster start. Her eyes are still closed. She doesn't want to come up short of the gate.

Beep.

Her fingers grab the sled tighter. The toes in her boots curl as they try to grip extra hard on the forest floor. She pulls herself forward again.

Beep.

Her heels dig into the dirt and she extends her back. The front of the sled lifts off the ground. She gulps for air and opens her eyes wide.

Beep.

She slams her shoulders forward and squeezes her calf muscles as hard as she can to propel forward. The back of the sled leaps off the ground. The runners are entirely in the air. Spectra can't tell if she is flying or jumping or just imagining the gap between herself and the ground. *Maybe it is magic.*

The sled angles downward toward the gate.

Beep. Her mind plays the last sound. The crowd is silent. Then they are roaring.

Spectra's diaphragm expands and her stomach floats. Her breathing halts.

Trees are rushing past her.

The gate is growing in her field of view.

The wind on her face is causing a stream of tears out the far sides of her eyes.

Spectra thinks she's flying until she gets bumped. Her right butt cheek reverberates with shock.

The sled evens out. Maybe it was just uneven ground. She thinks she must still be flying because the sled starts picking up more speed.

The silver structure is roaring toward her.

The rest of Fourier Woods becomes a blur.

There's a whirring sound as the cool air rushes past her ears. She can hear just how fast she's going, even as her eyelids struggle to stay open.

Spectra slides right through the Gate of Splitsies and crashes on the other side.

15

Spectra opens her eyes and looks down at the leaves and dirt she landed in. Her limbs are kinked in every direction. There's mud above her left eyebrow and a leaf stuck to the mud. She extends her legs, then her arms. They still move.

She sees the Magic Sled of Nir. It looks unscathed. Did it just float the whole way?

Spectra starts wiping the grime off her legs and face and then the back-sides of her arms. She does what she can, but she's still a mess. Her parents would definitely know that she snuck out if they were to see her now.

I didn't want to look pretty today, she thinks to herself in disgust of all the mud on her face.

She rolls over and something catches her eye.

There's a second Spectra!

Her head jolts back in shock. The other Spectra also jolts back in shock.

The ground below her appears to be separated. It stretches in two different directions, each a similar path, and each one contains a Spectra.

She is split in two!

Spectra's mind is racing. She has already checked her arms and legs, but now she does an inner check. *Breathing?*

Good. Heart pumping? Good. Brain function? Unsure.

She's fully intact. There's just a second copy of her right in front of her eyes.

She is encountering herself from outside herself. The new perspective is freeing. She turns to one side then the other. She finds pieces of mud by looking across at the other version of herself rather than down at herself. After looking a little more, she decides that she looks prettier with the mud. Mirrors and cameras have been lying to her. She's less judgmental of her own looks. She sees herself as a separate person rather than a focal point at the command center of a body; a person who looks natural with mud everywhere.

Spectra feels confident.

Alice fell through the looking glass into a different world. Narnia only existed beyond the wardrobe. There's a whole Monster's, Inc. factory beyond the portal of Pixar. Spectra travelled through a portal, but she isn't in a different world, or at least it doesn't feel like it. There are two matching paths, but they aren't of a different fiber than the world she came from — the world of Ivv.

I was expecting something weird, she thinks.

She's not impressed. As far as magic realms go, Spectra has high standards. She has read enough books to know that there should be a Cheshire cat or an armored polar bear or something.

A fly buzzes past her right ear.

She turns her head.

She notices the other Spectra also turns.

So that's it, huh? I fall through a magic portal and all I get is a buzzing fly? Lame.

This is too confusing, she thinks. *There's two of me, we share our thoughts, and yet we have different bodies. "Other Spectra" is confusing when we both think it.*

Spectra decides that she must give names to each of her

avatars. This would allow her to distinguish each one in her thoughts.

Her first idea is to name them after Hogwarts houses. Gryffindor is the obvious choice, but perhaps too obvious, she decided. She knows that she can't possibly be associated with Slytherin, despite any similarities with ninjas. Ravenclaw and Hufflepuff are underused in a way that Gryffindor was not, and she is okay being associated with them. She doesn't know which avatar should be named after each house, but she decides they are good names. Hufflepuff works hard and they are loyal. She could be both those things. And Ravenclaw is smart and witty. She decides that she is definitely that too.

She decides to change up the names. Instead of Harry Potter, she could name the avatars after cookies. *Chocolate chip, thin mint, sugar… hmmm.* Spectra settles on Snickerdoodle and Macaroon. She likes the names.

What if I combined the names?

Snickerdoodle Hufflepuff and Macaroon Ravenclaw.

Both Spectras smile.

Snick and Mac for short, she thinks.

After some deep thinking, she decides that Snickerdoodle Hufflepuff is the avatar headed to the left and Macaroon Ravenclaw is the avatar headed to the right.

One path leads to Refarm and the other path leads to Fomacula. She is confident of this. It was written in *The Smoke of the Sinister* and so far, everything in there has come true. She just doesn't know which path is which.

Both Spectras, Snick and Mac, take a step. They each go down their own paths.

As she looks ahead, Snick doesn't see much down her path. Both paths have canopy cover like a guided tunnel, but the path on the left feels empty. The path on the right feels full of adventure.

If Spectra had the ability to choose, she would pick the path on the right. She would live her life as an adventure if she could. *Mac may be lucky. Boring paths are the worst.*

The side of each path is thick with brush. It wouldn't be easy to wander away from the path. Spectra reflects on this and decides she must stay totally internal to each of the paths. It is already enough of an adventure she's on; she doesn't need to get derailed in the woods.

Snick and Mac spot a sign with some writing at the intersection of the two paths. They walk over and find a poem reminiscent of Robert Frost's *The Road Not Taken*:

Two paths diverged in a silver gate,
And surprised I could still travel both
And be two travelers, short I did wait
And looked down both as far as I could
To where it bent in the undergrowth;

Then saw them both, as just as fair,
And having perhaps the equal claim,
Except it was different through the air;
Though as for that the phase shift there
Had not reflected them the same,

And both that morning equally lay
In eaves no beam left hidden black.
Oh, I saw the first and second today!
Yet knowing how ray interfered ray,
I measured the path length travelling back.

Dispersed by wave from whence an eye
Somewhere below the surface hence:
Two paths diverged in a gate, and I—
I took the chance both traveled by,
And saw in fringes all the difference.

16

Each Spectra, Snick and Mac, grabs the Magic Sled of Nir that exists in her own path. It feels real in each instance. They walk up the other side of the dell to the top of a knoll and look back. In shared thought, Spectra figures that the Magic Sled of Nir doesn't need to come with her on the next part of her journey. It took her through the Gate of Splitsies, but that was its utility in this world. Snick and Mac each find a large matching mockernut hickory tree to set the matching sleds behind. They prop the sleds up against the trunk of each tree. The sleds both scrape some of bark off and then stabilize.

The Spectras return to the path and confirm that both sleds are sufficiently hidden. This is equally true for both paths. The thoughts from both Spectras are shared. Observations can be compared from one path to the other, but there is only one thought at a time. As Snickerdoodle Hufflepuff thinks about cookies, Macaroon Ravenclaw also thinks about cookies. But if one Spectra were to see a cookie and the other did not, they both could grasp the comparison between the wonderful and sad paths.

Having gone through the Gate of Splitsies and having not been cut in half, the shared mind of Spectra starts thinking about how lucky she is again. She decides this is extrinsic luck. Spectra happened to find a sled that didn't cut her in half when it divided in two. That was very fortunate.

As a tool, she wonders what else she could use the sled for.

Suppose I carried a cookie with me through the Gate of Splitsies, she thinks.

Just the thought of a warm sugary crumbly cookie makes her mouth water.

Would I end up with two cookies? Could I eat both cookies?

Mac thinks about Snick. She gets a weird protectionist jealousy when she realizes that Snick would be the holder of her other cookie. Mac would need to distract Snick and ninja the cookie away from her. But Snickerdoodle Hufflepuff is, as the saying goes, a smart cookie. Snick realizes that Mac is thinking about stealing a cookie from her and starts thwarting Mac's plan. The ability to share knowledge makes it impossible to scheme against each other.

Snick and Mac start scheming together as Spectra again.

If I took the cookies around and went through the Gate of Splitsies a second time, could I then make four cookies? Would they double exponentially until I had a whole batch of cookies for myself, err myselves?

It delights Spectra to think about all the cookies.

Snick and Mac walk down each path equally. Hiking two trails at once is mentally taxing for the shared mind of Spectra, but she can handle it because the trails aren't difficult to hike. In Mac's path, there's the faint sound of music coming through the trees. Snick's path is silent.

Spectra recalls playing *Zelda: Breath of the Wild*. Kass, a giant minstrel bird from Rito played an accordion along various paths. *Breath of the Wild* is Spectra's favorite video game of all time. Using the accordion for echolocation, Spectra would find Kass. Kass would tell informative tales about the history of Hyrule. It was delightful and serene to hear the accordion. Then, after listening to Kass, Spectra would go beat up some baddies before the blood moon rose once again.

Accordion players on a hiking trail are not unique to video games. At both ends of the #2 hiking trail in the Cinque Terre between Monterosso al Mare and Vernazza, hikers are often enchanted by accordion players sitting under the rows of grape vines. It's one of the more pleasant forms of busking. The rising sound of music helps to mark the end of a good hiking leg.

Mac can't see where the music is coming from, but she appreciates the way "Here Comes the Sun" by the Beatles gets louder as she approaches. There's a boulder in the path with the accordion that she climbs over.

She finds two boys, one with an accordion and the other there by his side to help.

"Hi there," she says.

"Well hi," the second one says as the first continues to play. "Beautiful day out, isn't it?"

"Yes. I suppose so," Mac says with a look of hesitation on her face.

"Are you lost?" asks the second one.

The accordion-playing boy stops playing.

"No, I'm not lost. I'm just on an adventure. My name's Spec—err Mac; what's yours?"

While Mac is talking with the accordion boys, Snick is still blissfully hiking.

"I'm Poselem and this here is my brother Negelem," one of the boys says to Mac.

The one with the accordion, Negelem, is short and stout. His brother, Poselem, is quite a bit taller and skinnier. They are simple looking boys.

"What brings you 'round these parts?" Poselem asks.

"I'm looking for Refarm and Fomacula," Mac says.

"Do you know where those are?"

"Well you're on the right path for Fomacula," says Poselem.

"But I've never heard of Refarm," says Negelem.

"Well, you don't get out much," says Poselem.

"I don't really have to," says Negelem.

Mac's eyes dart back and forth as the conversation is already derailed. She needs these boys to stay within the red lines.

"Boys, could we focus a little?" Mac says in frustration. "That's N/A to my situation here."

If two boys argue in the woods and nobody is around to hear it, do they argue right past each other?

Mac continues, "Sorry. I'm not trying to be rude, but I kind of really need to save the world from this fog and get back before dinner if I ever want to eat a cookie again."

The brothers look at each other in surprise and shame.

"That sounds serious!" Negelem says.

"It is. It's very important," Mac says, a little defiant and indignant.

Spectra considers that while Mac is talking with the boys, Snick is continuing down her path. The two Spectras are both trying to hike to the end of their paths, but they are not beholden to the same phases of delay. Snick may walk one unimpeded, and Mac might be slowed in the other path.

"Fomacula is straight ahead," Poselem points.

Mac is headed toward Fomacula, Spectra thinks, *and Snick must be headed to Refarm. I know where both versions of me are going.*

"What's Fomacula like?" Mac asks.

"Oh, we don't really go that way," says Negelem.

"Yeah, I heard it might be dangerous," says Poselem. "Or weird. I don't really know. In fact, did I hear that from you, Negelem?"

"Oh no. I didn't say anything," says Negelem.

The sun is high overhead. A few rays are peaking

through the canopy and streaming down to the detritus on the hiking trail. Dust floats in and out of the beams, giving an ethereal feel to the woods. It must be approaching midday by the angle of the rays.

"So, neither of you have been to Fomacula?" asks Mac.

They look embarrassed. Poselem turns to Negelem with his lips furled. The look of shame that Negelem gives him in return causes laughter.

"Well, I guess not!" says Poselem, though giggles.

Hmmm, Mac mumbles.

"Where'd you hear about Fomacula anyway?" Negelem asks. "It's not exactly a popular tourist destination this time of year."

"How would you know?" Mac asks. "You said you've never been."

"Well, I mean," Negelem tries to contort his face into a plausible answer, "it's just something I've heard. Just a joke, you know."

Mac squints her eyes. She's trying to read them properly. "I…" she hesitates, "read about it in a book."

"Oh, yes, yes," Poselem says. "*37 More Fun Things to Do in Fomacula* is one of the best travel memoirs of all time."

"Poselem lent it to me last year," Negelem says. "You'll never believe number 12!"

Mac is starting to get annoyed. "It wasn't that book," she says.

"You must have read the original!" says Poselem, excitedly.

"I've heard good things about the first 63 things you can do," adds Negelem. "What did you think? I haven't read it yet."

Mac can tell that these boys don't quite have their magnets aligned.

"It was a *different* book," she stresses.

"What was it called?" asks Poselem. "I like books about Fomacula."

"Yeah me too!" adds Negelem. "What was it called…

for me too?"

Mac thinks about this. She knows the brothers are well-meaning, but it would probably cause quite the ruckus if she told them the real name of the book.

"It was called…" Mac pauses, "*An Additional 98 More Things That Happen in Fomacula.*" She is pleased with herself when she says it. She even cracks a smirk.

"Oh, that just sounds wonderful!" Poselem says.

"Yeah!" agrees Negelem. "We'll have to look for it. Thanks so much for the recommendation!"

"You're welcome," Mac says. She sees her opening and seizes it. "If I want to get to thing number 81, I really need to get a move on."

"Ooooh, thing number 81." Negelem says.

"I hear that's the best one," Poselem says. "We can definitely do that one first when we visit."

Sometimes the end of a conversation drags. The person trying to leave realizes that it's over, but others may not. The brothers are oblivious and could talk for hours if Mac let them. Instead, she uses the opportunity to be curt with them.

She curls a strand of hair back over her ear and grabs the straps on her backpack. "Thanks again," she says with a smile. She starts walking toward Fomacula.

Behind her, Mac can hear the chatter as the two brothers discuss visiting Fomacula. Her eyes are fixed forward. She has a mission to accomplish. After a few seconds, the accordion starts playing again.

The song is "Somewhere Over the Rainbow."

17

Mac happens upon a bend in the path to Fomacula. It's a strong right angle. At the vertex of the bend is a sign. It's a large golden metallic sign, the color of Notre Dame's football helmets. The sign sits on a wooden post and the juxtaposition of the natural wood and the shiny polished golden sign makes Mac uneasy.

The sign is blank.

It's shaped like an elongated rectangular stop sign. The cut off corners give it a softer feel and the edges have been sanded down so that they aren't as sharp as the material would imply.

Mac can see herself in the reflection when she looks at it dead on.

She backs up in the path and realizes that it isn't just the reflection of herself that she can see, but also the path. Each direction comes in at a forty-five-degree angle, so she is able to use it like a rounded garage mirror.

Mac doesn't know why such a thing would exist, let alone exist in this particular location. The sign is polished. It's clearly man-made and deliberately placed. Yet, it doesn't have any text on it. Is it supposed to have text on it? Did somebody install it in an unfinished state?

She peers around to the backside of the sign. No text.

It's mysterious.

Mac wonders, *Can a sign have a purpose if it has no text, no images, no indication of intent?*

She considers that it's just a marker to let her know that she's still on the trail. She has seen trees with trail markers and small wooden posts marking trails, but not a golden sign. She has even seen stacked rocks indicate a path.

This sign just doesn't look like it's a trail marker.

She taps it with her fingers. It clinks.

Mac figures that some mysteries in life are better left unsolved. She turns and continues down the path.

Two girls are standing together.

Mac doesn't want another long conversation like she had with Negelem and Poselem, but she feels compelled to be friendly to the girls nonetheless.

"Good afternoon," Mac says.

"Greetings!" they say in unison.

Mac looks back and forth between the two. They must be sisters. "Do you know what's up with that golden sign back there?"

"It's very shiny, isn't it?" says the first girl.

"Yes, but why is it there?" asks Mac.

"They probably couldn't find a better place for it," says the second girl.

"No. But like, why does it even exist?" Mac asks. "There are no words on it. The question isn't 'why there', but 'why anywhere?' What purpose does it serve?"

"Good point," says the first one.

"Yes. Quite astute," says the second.

"I'm Annabel," says the first girl with an outstretched hand.

"And I'm Brianna," says the second.

Mac isn't happy that her question was ignored but pressing the matter won't make the girls know why the sign exists. "Are you—" Mac starts to ask.

Annabel interrupts. "Yes!"

"That's weird because I met two brothers just back that way," Mac points.

"Yes, but we're not just sisters," says Brianna. "Can't you tell that we look alike?"

"Oh! You're twins," Mac says in astonishment.

"Not just twins," Annabel says. Then Brianna joins in as well and they both say, "we're triplets!"

Mac stares at them. She counts two of them. It was weird when she encountered the brothers, but now she is wondering if it's not just her that is split in two. Or three, for that matter, even though she doesn't see a third sister.

"There's only two of you though," Mac points out.

"Ahh. Well, yes," Brianna says. "Joanna is right around the corner."

Mac looks ahead on the path to where Brianna points. She can't see the third triplet. She does notice another one of the golden signs, however.

"There!" Mac points ahead. "See. It's another one of those golden signs. It's right there."

"Would you look at that!" says Annabel.

Mac realizes that she isn't going to get an answer about the signs. She decides she's curious about something else though. "Your names. Don't they seem a little bit similar?"

"Well, what's your name then?" asks Brianna.

The deflection throws Mac off. "I'm Macaroon Ravenclaw," she says.

"That sounds like a fake name," Brianna says.

"You can call me Mac."

"Peculiar," Brianna says. "Very peculiar."

"See," Annabel says to Brianna. "Luanna was right!"

"Wait," Mac says. "Are you messing with me right now? Who is Luanna?"

Both girls gasp.

"Luanna had some issues," Brianna says. "We loved her like a sister, but she got out of line. She lost focus and couldn't conform. She's in quarantine."

Mac doesn't know who 'they' are, and she is too afraid to ask. She also doesn't understand what they mean by quarantine, but she thinks it sounds like a friendship quarrel that doesn't interest her.

"We know better than to step out of line," adds Annabel.

"Conformity is our normity," says Brianna.

Mac isn't sure what to do with that. On the one hand, focus is good. It's nearly impossible to accomplish anything of value without incredibly precise focus. On the other hand, she thinks adventure paralysis is keeping them from experiencing the world. Shouldn't they want to do more with their lives?

"So, what are you doing out here then?" Mac asks.

"We wanted to get some pictures out in nature," says Annabel.

"Profile pictures," says Brianna.

"Like for the internet?" Mac asks.

"For our social lives," says Annabel. "And we can time-release the pictures over the next year to make it look like we come out here all the time. The lighting is interesting, and the fog makes it seem mysterious."

Mac thinks for a moment then says, "You're just here to get… selfies?"

"Oh no," says Brianna. "We aren't that vain. Annabel is taking my picture."

Spectra suddenly feels pride in the mud on her face. On both of her faces, Mac's and Snick's. It feels good to get dirty and accomplish something. She likes pointing her camera toward the things she finds interesting as well, but she doubts that her photography portfolio would have much overlap with theirs.

"I've got a lot of followers," says Annabel.

Spectra doesn't have any followers.

"I'm going to get paid as an influencer," says Brianna.

Oprah is an influencer. Spectra cares what she has to say. She doesn't care what these girls have to say, so she decides to be more tactful. "You have gorgeous skin."

"I knew it!" Annabel says. "You are jealous of my beauty."

"Our beauty," Brianna says.

"Envy," Mac corrects.

"Admitting it too," Annabel says,

Mac smiles. The mud on her face is freeing her from what little she may have cared. This is a game now to her. "Caught me! Haha. You two are so smart too!"

Annabel and Brianna start to smile. They feel good about themselves.

"I hope you don't get mud on your faces like I did," Mac says. "I had to put my phone away. It's pretty much, like, the worst thing ever."

"It does sound bad," says Annabel. "Aren't you bored?"

"Very yes!" Mac says. "I don't know what to do with myself."

"You could clean yourself up and put on some makeup." Annabel says. "It worked wonders on Brianna."

"You're the one that needs to clean up!" Brianna retorts.

Spite grows on their faces. Mac can see the self-destructive competition forming. They might spend their whole lives in a battle to do less, just to claim they have fewer scratches on their skin than the other. Mac sees this as her cue to leave.

"It was so wonderful meeting you beautiful women," Mac says with a smile. "but I don't have the strong will required to stay pristinely still like the two of you. I must be on my way."

The sisters break their intense competition to say goodbye.

"It was wonderful to meet you too!" says Annabel with a genuine smile.

"The pleasure was all mine!" says Brianna with a wink.

Mac turns and continues down the path to Fomacula.

Her boots don't match her skirt. There's wind in her face and an adventure to be had.

The second golden sign looks nearly identical to the first. It barely warrants an inspection as Mac passes it. The path bends at another right angle.

Joanna is picking at a flower when Mac sees her.

"You must be Joanna!" Mac says.

"That's me. Did you meet my sisters?" Joanna says.

"Oh yes. They were lovely people. And so incredibly beautiful too! Your family has such wonderful skin."

"Why, thank you!"

"And that flower is so pretty. Are you going to put it in your hair?"

"Yes. Yes, I am. My sisters would never come over here to pick a flower, but that's why I'm going to be the most beautiful."

Mac smiles and says with a whisper, "It's working." She winks.

Joanna lights up in delight.

"Hey, you wouldn't happen to know what's down this path, would you?" Mac asks.

"Oh yes. If you keep going, you'll enter the rare bee expanse."

"Well, I'll be." Mac says.

"It's far too dangerous to go in, but you can find flowers growing outside the expanse like I did," Joanna adds.

"I'm not doing too much today," Mac says, "I think I might go check it out."

Joanna give Mac a confused look. She can't comprehend somebody wanting to enter the expanse.

"Thank you!" Mac says.

"You… are welcome," replies Joanna.

Mac keeps walking straight toward the rare bee expanse.

18

The rare bee expanse smells like vanilla and lavender.

The entrance is flanked on either side by colorful blooming azaleas and rhododendrons. Mac can't tell if the fog is lighter in the rare bee expanse or if the colorful flowers just make it seem less dull and dreary.

A honeybee flies past her ear.

Mac flinches.

There's a large fuzzy black bumblebee buzzing around her right shin.

Mac makes a conscious effort to avoid kicking it.

A Melipona with a large looking stinger lands on her arm.

Mac's heart is racing.

She doesn't realize it, but Meliponas are stingless bees.

The Melipona flies off to pollinate an azalea.

Mac takes a deep breath. She can feel the blood rushing through her arteries. It is filled with adrenaline. Her defense mechanisms kick in as she feels the throbbing intensity of the danger of her location.

Mac starts to wonder about the name. *Is it rare because there aren't many bee expanses, or does it contain rare bees?*

Cute and cuddly furry animals often get their own wildlife preserves. Creatures that can defend themselves, like bees, don't. It's unfortunate because flowers and fruit need bees to become pollinated. The world needs bees. Maybe this sanctuary is key to their survival.

Mac realizes that she has entered their land. She is just a visitor and it is her duty to respect her surroundings.

She starts to think about collecting. If this rare bee expanse is the work of somebody's deliberate collection, it must be impressive. Stamps or beanie babies or coins or Pokémon and other collectables are simply better, more valuable, as the collection grows. What makes a collection valuable isn't an individual rare item, but that it is collected and contrasted with other rare and common items. The whole is better than the original.

Maybe it is part of human nature to organize things. Collections are just groupings of organized objects, or in this case, animals. We find beauty in the organization, even beyond the beauty itself.

Would a single Monet be impressive? Would it become famous? Or is it possible that his interpretation, his art style, applied to waterlilies and haystacks alike makes the artwork more about the style or aesthetics than about the objects portrayed?

Michelangelo's *David* and the ceiling of the Sistine Chapel are not only made with different media, but they are also different in style. However, as Michelangelo was the master of the human form, maybe even those disparate works lend strength to each other.

The collection Spectra is currently walking through, the rare bee expanse, is a work of art in its own right. Nature preserves are museums which are indistinguishable from magic in the artful realm of the wild. They become more interesting than the sum of their individual pieces in the same way that an art collection builds upon itself. If this bee expanse is home to many types of bees, then it is a rare beauty.

Mac enters a field of goldenrod. The bees couldn't be happier to land on the petals and pistils. The fog has a slight green tint in the field of goldenrod, as pollen fills the air. The smell of flowers is intense and calming.

As she walks, Mac becomes less tense.

The rare bee expanse grows on her as a concept.

Mac starts to smile. She becomes happy being among all the bees. They are delighted to have this place to call their own. No longer does she see them as a threat to her, but rather that she is a threat to them.

She treads lightly through the trail.

The wide-open fields of flowers feel airy. The woods recede behind her. She can feel the connection with the sun, even with the fog scattering the warm rays.

Mac decides she's no longer afraid of bees. She decides that they deserve our love.

On the path ahead, Mac sees a break in the fog. There's a wide stream of light pouring through the clouds.

The bees stop following her. She decides she must have exited their preserve.

Spectra considers her journey. All the excitement has occurred to Mac in the path to Fomacula. Snick has not had any excitement or diversions on the path to Refarm. The two paths may both take time to traverse, and they may match in length, but they differ in the obstacles dispersed along the way.

At the break in the clouds, Mac feels heat reentering her body. Her skin warms to a soft glow. She feels rejuvenated in her quest. It's amazing: there's a giant ball of nuclear fusion almost a hundred million miles away that forms an unimpeded straight line through the break in the fog. Light from the sun streams in little packets of energy down to the surface of the Earth, and they wave as they pass.

Mac looks down toward the ground. There's a wide

hole in the ground where those waving rays from the sun should hit.

It can't be coincidence. There must be a reason for the break in the fog directly above the hole in the ground.

Mac gets excited.

She approaches the hole. From the rim she sees up through the clouds. The sun is shining brightly in a pale blue sky that she hasn't seen in over a month. The sight is so beautiful, or maybe so bright, it almost brings her to tears.

She looks down into the deep hole. She knows it's where she must go.

19

Mac climbs into the hole.

She doesn't have a rope to help her rappel down. It isn't safe. Mac doesn't care. Sometimes a girl must step outside her comfort zone if she hopes to accomplish great things.

The light from the sun feels intense on her back as she descends. It feels strange after so long in the fog. Her skin tingles with confusion as the UV rays prick at her cells. She wishes she had brought sunscreen with her, although she had no way to know she would need it.

Her hands get sweaty as she grabs the sidewall.

Her concentration intensifies.

She didn't come all this way to just slip down some hole. She's not going to let go with her fingertips.

The temperature rises as she descends. It starts to become muggy and thick in the air. There's something interesting about moving from the high humidity of the fog, where the water droplets cool her skin, to the high humidity of the new biome which is sticky and stagnant, and causes sweat to bead on her lower back.

Her forearms are aching once again. The day has been a workout.

She finds the lower edge of the sidewall and pauses.

It's a drop down to the ground.

Mac isn't a fan of heights. She seems to put herself in situations that require her to overcome this fear, but it is still there. She looks down. It's too far.

She closes her eyes and concentrates. There are two options. She could give up and climb back up the sidewall or she can drop down.

Without even thinking through which option she wants to take, her fingers slip. A whole colony of butterflies swirl around in her stomach. She plummets downward.

One time, Spectra and her friend Crystal were standing in an elevator with mirrored walls. The right angles of the mating surfaces were doing something interesting. Crystal pointed out that if she looked at the corner of the elevator, where the two walls and the ceiling met, her head was always centered in that very spot. She moved her head, but her right eye remained locked there. Spectra was confused. When she looked at the corner, she saw her own eye, not Crystal's. Spectra tried to move off the corner as well, but she could always see her own eye at that very spot. They both started bobbing up and down, left and right. The elevator door opened behind them and a confused on-looker saw them dancing for their reflections.

Snick, at the end of the path to Refarm, experiences this same sensation once again. She sees three mirrors form a retroreflector, just like the walls of the elevator. After the long path of boring nothingness to Refarm, the end leaves her staring directly back at herself. It's like a sick joke. The only decoration is a large flag. She tries to duck out of the vertex, but her head remains fixed in place. The walls seem alive. The walls seem magical. The magic in the walls is enough to thwart even the craftiest ninja.

Mac falls from the sidewall of the hole she was descending. Her arms rise in the air with inertia as her torso plummets to Earth.

There's a wet surface below that has some bounce.

She falls on her back and flings forward up toward her feet. The soles of her boots don't grip the surface and she continues her rotation straight back onto her face. She puts her arms out. They break the fall, but only so much. Mac is laying still. She can feel her neck from the whiplash of the landing, but she decides it isn't broken and she stands back up.

She glances around at her new environment. She's standing in what appears to be a large smooth bowl. The surface is made of some sort of a webbed red net. There are bright red arroyos of flowing fluid underneath the surface. She feels uneasy in the new biome. This isn't a place she's ever read about in the library.

Mac looks up and sees the hole that she fell through. It looks like the Pantheon in Rome. It's stunning. Light streams in through the hole in a cone shape down to a single point in the red net. It forms an intensely bright spot on the ground. *Doesn't light usually stream through the sky in cylinders?* Mac thinks.

As Mac starts walking around, she notes that the ground feels like a cross between a trampoline park and a pit of mud with Saran Wrap over the top. When she steps on the veins of the red net, she feels a sturdy taught halyard underneath. The give and bounce of the ground makes the new biome a sensationally fun destination.

There's some topography to the fun destination too. The red net of faux vias emerge from a mound and form tributaries that recombine with increasing width at a glowing disc that makes Mac nervous.

As Mac continues to look around, she notices that she can see through the surface of the red net ground. There are so many layers. The fun destination is spongey and squishy with layer upon layer of padding.

There's a second mound in the periphery of Mac's

vision. It looks like there is a smoky splatter underneath the mound. Last weekend, when Liam's friend Mason smashed a Halloween pumpkin, he made an organic splatter mess. If that splatter had been in space, it would have spread out in all directions. This is what Mac sees. She sees the three-dimensional explosion of a fruit, splaying and spraying every which way.

Given the red color of the splatter, Mac decides it looks like a blast tomato.

She examines the rest of the red net and decides that the blast tomato is the culprit for the fog in the village of Ivv. Nothing else is as obviously wrong as the blast tomato beneath the red net surface.

She's overcome with joy. This is Fomacula. She set out to find it and here she is, the end of her journey. Relief flows through her body and loosens her posture.

The mystery is solved. Mac knows what she must do.

She must remove the blast tomato to free the village of Ivv from the oppressive fog that's causing cranky pants to be worn throughout.

A sinking feeling forms in Mac's gut.

She has no idea how to do it. She doesn't know how to remove a blast tomato.

In her bag is a water bottle and nothing else of use. This is not a job for a bottle of water. Mac came all this way on her adventure and she wasn't prepared for the task at hand.

Her enthusiasm fades.

That was a tad presumptuous, she thinks. *This is not a job for just one person. Especially not one person with only her two hands and no tools. I was not prepared for this.*

A single tear forms in her left eye.

Her bottom lip puckers and quivers.

She sinks down to the ground, proud of how far she has come, but unprepared emotionally to handle the weight of what comes next.

Spectra's favorite tennis star, Caroline Wozniacki, had

been the #1 ranked women's tennis player in world for a long time before she finally won her first grand slam event. When she finally did break through and win the 2018 Australian Open, she wasn't prepared for the emotional weight of her accomplishment. She laid on her back on the tennis court, having finally achieved her ultimate goal, only to feel as though she had taken but one step in her grand adventure. Mac feels exactly like Caroline.

Her jaw goes slack.

The scope of the task is more than she can handle alone.

She needs help to remove the blast tomato and clear the smoke of the sinister. She knows she must return to Ivv and regroup with the right tools and a capable team. She hates asking for help. It feels like failure to her. She swallows her pride. Mac now knows it's the only way for her to succeed.

20

When the hill becomes too steep
Leaving your quadriceps to ache
Leading anguish to a weep
It's more than you can take

Be a mighty mountain goat
Push past the lowly sheep
The mountain becomes of note
When the hill becomes too steep

Mac takes in a deep breath and then exhales. She does it again with her eyes closed. Her arms are wrapped in a hugging embrace of her own torso. She picks herself up emotionally by reminding herself that only the difficult tasks are worth pursuit. *I must go back to Ivv for more resources. There's no way to remove the blast tomato by myself.*

She finds a wall that she can climb out of Fomacula and starts ascending.

It feels… cathartic.

In Refarm, Snickerdoodle Hufflepuff also turns around, sick of looking at herself and the flag in the retroreflector. Both avatars of Spectra are heading back toward the Couplera Gate, if they can find it.

The Fomacula sidewall is organic enough for Mac to dig her fingers into while she's in the lower biome of the open dome. It becomes rigid, but uneven enough to function like a rock-climbing wall as she reenters the environment that she knows. It takes all her strength to climb out, but she is filled with adrenaline and focused on her plan.

Mac pulls herself up out of the hole.

What she thought would feel like failure, after returning to solid ground, feels reassuring. She didn't want to walk back through the rare bee expanse while the fog was still there, but she nonetheless feels comforted by knowing what lays ahead.

Season 34 of the TV show Survivor was called Game Changers. It was a season of returning players. The three players to make final tribal council were Troyzan, Culpepper, and Sarah. Troyzan was outwardly nice and inwardly nice throughout the game. The jury ignored him entirely, knowing he wasn't at all a ninja. He received zero votes in Survivor: Game Changers. Culpepper was both outwardly sly and inwardly sly. It was an arrogant game that lacked social awareness. Some members of the jury respected his approach, but it was largely interpreted as bullyish. He received three votes. Sarah was outwardly nice and inwardly sly. She once said, "I only trust myself." She's a real ninja. She knew that she needed to use her social game to woo her competitors and she had to use her intelligence to be smart in how she played them. That's why Sarah won Survivor: Game Changers.

Spectra doesn't like that she must win others over to complete her mission, but she knows that a good ninja, like Sarah was, needs to work with others. Spectra had been too much like Culpepper. That's why she failed on the first try.

Mac tries to internalize what she has learned. Ninjas are

smart about being sly.

Maybe the fog clouded my judgment, she thinks.

No worries. She is moving on. She is learning lessons and becoming a better ninja with every adventure.

Mac speeds through the rare bee expanse without stopping to smell the flowers. Since she knows the way, it goes quickly.

Joanna is still in the path, just beyond the expanse, but she's distracted by another flower, and Mac passes by unnoticed. Brianna and Annabel are busy taking pictures of themselves as Mac sneaks right past them as well. As a ninja, Mac would appreciate if her job was a little bit more difficult. She didn't go to three years of ninja homeschool to just be ignored without trying to be stealthy. Mac realizes that the girls are only in the woods to take pictures of themselves to post onto Instapound. It feels like a misuse of the woods to Mac. Nature is for hiking, not for glamour shots. Adventures are not made online.

There was a famous Stanford marshmallow experiment. Professor Walter Mischel conducted a series of tests on delayed gratification in young children. He found that years later, the children who were able to delay gratification had more successful lives. It has proven to be one of the most predictive developmental indicators in human development. Social media is basically a digital marshmallow. The girls focus on their Instapound accounts and lose all determination and purpose. Mac feels sorry for them. If they only weren't so concerned about what other people thought, they could go on awesome ninja adventures to interesting places.

Mac passes Poselem and Negelem. The boys are arguing back and forth about which places they want to go to. She knows they will never visit those places. They lack vision. They spend so much energy coming up with ideas, but execution is what really matters. Mac wishes that Negelem would go back to playing the accordion. *Stay in focus*, she reminds herself. She isn't on a vacation either;

she's on a mission.

When Mac returns all the way to find the Magic Sled of Nir, it is still propped up against the tree, where she left it. Snick finds her sled too.

Now I must find the Couplera Gate, both Spectras think.

Snickerdoodle Hufflepuff and Macaroon Ravenclaw are both on top of the knoll looking down the dell to the Gate of Splitsies. They have returned at the same time.

This must be the Eli Manning kind of luck, intrinsic luck. The paths, one to Refarm and one to Fomacula, are exactly the same length. It's a lucky coincidence owing to the nature of each path. It seems especially lucky considering the extra time Mac spent talking with the boys and girls and exploring deep in Fomacula.

That says nothing about the lack of luck that Snick and Mac are experiencing in their quest to find the Couplera Gate.

They try to think back to *The Smoke of the Sinister*. It was a riddle back then and it isn't clearer now. Snick and Mac only know that they must use the Couplera Gate to recombine.

They each set their sled down and sit on it to contemplate.

Mac opens her backpack and grabs the bottle of water. It feels cool and refreshing. She hadn't realized how parched she had become. When somebody is intensely focused on a task they are said to be in flow. Mac was in an adventure flow. Now she is letting the water flow.

Wolf creek rushes past, reminding her that she is almost back home.

Mac thinks about magic, because that is what she needs to use right now. The Harry Potter books are the best reference manuals of all time for understanding magic, so she thinks about those.

The swirl of water in Wolf Creek relaxes Mac's mind. It makes her feel uninhibited.

Mac starts to think about the water in Wolf Creek.

There's a charm in Harry Potter called *Aqua Eructo*, used to shoot water from a wand. There's also a spell called *Aguamenti* that does pretty much the same thing. *Impervius* makes an object repel water.

Snick and Mac both spring to their feet.

The Couplera Gate, both Spectras think, *must be the Gate of Splitsies if taken in reverse.*

Magic is a two-way gate, just like luck. And it can have two names for the same object. That's just how magic works. It's part of what obfuscates the very nature of magic. If magic weren't a riddle, nobody would be a muggle.

Snick and Mac each grab their Magic Sleds of Nir, back up, and get a running start toward the crest of the hill. They fling themselves head first down the dell without looking or examining the track and fly down the dell with abandon.

They are dead center as they ride through the gate.

21

Spectra lands the dismount like Simone Biles.

The sled is tilted up and Spectra is leaning back with the pull of gravity. Before falling backward, she puts her left foot onto the ground and stands straight up. She looks back over her shoulder and down at the ground. She scans behind the trees and decides she's alone. Snick and Mac have recombined. There's only one Spectra now. The gate, taken in reverse, is the Couplera Gate.

At the top of the dell, Spectra sets the sled against a tree for safe keeping again. It rests nicely against the trunk, and detritus and dirt curl up onto the back of the sled where it meets the ground. There's moss growing off the trail, underneath the ferns. Caterpillars crawl on large leaves.

Spectra hikes back down to Ivv with Wolf Creek by her side, guiding her back. Her boots are warming up from the friction of hiking and the sweat of midday.

It feels bright when she exits Fourier Woods, even with the heavy cover of fog. There's a wide plain of green below her and a featureless blur above. It feels so open that it's disorienting. On the path, she knew where to go; in this free space, she has a prism of choice. The ground has become directionless. There's more sky above than before. She squints her eyes.

She pauses. She raises her right hand and brushes her chin. Then she runs her fingers through her ponytail and flip it back.

Where to? she thinks.

Spectra surveys the village in front of her.

Each building houses different people that would interpret her findings differently. Each would add a layer of understanding to what she has seen. She could go to more houses to get more layers of nuance. The blast tomato is too urgent for that. The day is getting too late. So, she windows in on the most important building with the smartest people in town, the one that will interpret the fringe results with clinical precision. Spectra takes a step forward and sets out seeking the doctors.

Fercher Street, which bisects the village of Ivv, acts like a channel that divides two sides of a binned pair of buildings. Each front door faces another, perfectly. The flow of traffic, by motor or by foot, get the sense of comradery rather than rivalry. That happens with precision placement. One door on the left is sky blue and the other is white. Then a door is red, paired with black. Then a standard blue, together again with white. Take any two colors and pair them together, especially if one of the colors is a neutral black or white, and they will appear to match.

There are pumpkins in front of some of the doors. Spectra likes how the orange brings out the best in the color of the doors. Some go further and decorate with hay bales and scarecrows. One of the houses has spider webbing.

The storefronts in Ivv are in on the spirit too. They are decorated with cartoon skeletons holding up sale signs. For a moment, Spectra forgets that the decorations were installed with a sense of obligation rather than out of delight. The town feels magical in October, even as the fog makes the citizens feel depressed.

She finds Doctors Ophelia, Thelma, and Molly at the Toth Medical Center, busy with paperwork, but without a patient in sight.

"Hi," Spectra says as she approached the doctors.

Dr. Ophelia is an older, more experienced doctor. She has a deliberate way in which she moves. Dr. Thelma is a little younger and is comparably peppy, with a bright white set of teeth, almost always poking out. Dr. Molly is the youngest of the three. Her hair seems sculpted in place with perfection, and she looks into patient's hearts with warm, compassionate eyes when she talks. She's the first one to smile as she crouches down to greet Spectra on an equal level.

"Well, hello Spectra," she says. "How are you today?"

Dr. Thelma and Ophelia turn their heads.

"Good. I mean bad. I mean," Spectra says, overwhelmed by the question.

"Do you need us to bandage you up?" asks Dr. Molly. "It looks like you got a few cuts there."

Spectra looked down at her shins. She feels them now that Dr. Molly mentioned them, but she had forgotten about the pain when she was focused on Fomacula. "No," she says. "I need your help with something else."

Dr. Ophelia gives Dr. Thelma an inquisitive look. There's some worry on her face.

"Okay," Dr. Molly says. "What would you like me to help you with?"

"I found this blast tomato in this really weird place," Spectra says. "And I was split into two at the time. The fog was causing me all kinds of problems, so I found this book, and this sled, and this gate, and I was split into two, and discovered the blast tomato. I need your help to remove it.

"Hold on a second," says Dr. Thelma. "You were split

in two?"

"Oh, don't worry about that," Spectra says. "I'm in one piece again."

Dr. Molly leans slightly forward. "This blast tomato, how would you describe it?"

"It's so big. Like scraps of tomato spraying out. It was in Fomacula."

"How did you get there and where is it?" asks Dr. Molly.

"It was beyond the Gate of Splitsies. I rode the Magic Sled of Nir through the Gate of Splitsies and then hiked to the end. That's what the book told me to do."

"That sounds like a very interesting book, Spectra," Dr. Molly says.

"I found it at the library," Spectra says. "Like the sled. That was there too. They were in different places though. A super weird riddle book thingy said It would happen and then it did happen."

"How did you find a book like that?" asks Dr. Ophelia.

"I was grou—" Spectra almost slips. "great at figuring out where things are in the library. It's my favorite place."

"What was the book called?" asks Dr. Thelma.

"I was in the library and I needed to figure out how to get rid of this fog so that things go back to normal again," Spectra says.

"Yes, but did the book have a name?" asks Dr. Molly.

"*The Smoke of the Sinister.*"

"And it was about fog or smoke?" asks Dr. Thelma.

"It was a really big book," Spectra adds.

"What a fantastic adventure you read about," says Dr. Ophelia.

"It was all real."

"Including this *blast tomato*, whatever that is?"

"Dr. Ophelia," Dr. Molly says.

"Uh-huh," Spectra says. "With the Magic Sled of Nir, it said, I could go to Refarm and Fomacula to get rid of this fog. So, I found the sled and was going to clear the fog, but I needed help. I couldn't do it all by myself."

The doctors try to process the new information. The conversation reaches a brief pause.

Dr. Molly turns to Dr. Ophelia. "'Sinister' can also mean—"

"Epitheli—" says Dr. Thelma.

"It is!" says Dr. Molly.

"It has angiogen—" says. Dr. Themla.

"If the apoptosis progresses, we could code!" says Dr. Molly.

The doctors spring to action.

"We need a cryoge—" says Dr. Thelma

"On it," says Dr. Ophelia.

Dr. Thelma looks at Dr. Molly. "—and your largest vol—" she motions with her index finger and thumb.

"Ranibizumab," says Dr. Ophelia.

"With drip?" asks Dr. Molly.

"We need an intra-arterial inj—" says Dr. Thelma.

"Forceps too. Stat." says Dr. Ophelia.

Spectra is confused. They are doing serious adult talk, but it's a bunch of words thrown back and forth that she doesn't understand. The conversation feels like chaos.

"We need panretinal spot photocoag—" says Dr. Thelma.

Dr. Ophelia and Dr. Thelma rush off.

"Spectra," Dr. Molly says, "we think this might be serious. You did a great job figuring out the fog situation and now we need your help."

"Yes!" Spectra says.

"We need one more person to help us. Somebody that's good at climbing, maybe. Do you know anybody?"

"Uh-huh," Spectra says.

"Could you please go get them and meet us right back here?" asks Dr. Molly.

"Uh-huh."

"Hurry though," says Dr. Molly. "If what you say is true and it's what we think it might be, we aren't worried about the fog becoming permanent."

"You aren't?"

"No," says Dr. Molly. "We're worried the fog is just the start. We're worried that the world is going to forever go dark."

22

Spectra knows who she must recruit. Liam is really the right person for the job. He's trustworthy, and he loves climbing. She doesn't know where to find him, but she suspects that he'll be back home. After the chestnut tree incident, he probably wanted to hide indoors.

Spectra knows that the house might be guarded by her parents on the main level. It would be dangerous if she tries to re-enter through the front door. Hugh might be in the living room or the kitchen. He could even be outside gardening. Hugh loved to prune his favorite bushes out in the yard on sunny days, but hasn't been as enthusiastic about it since the fog moved in. Ruby could be on the couch.

I have to climb back up through the window, she thinks.

The village seems emptier than a normal Saturday, which allows Spectra to make her way back to her house without excessive caution.

She examines the drain pipe below her bedroom. It feeds into a muddy part of the yard. She wades through the mud to put her hands on the siding. Her boots get glommed with the dirtiest gloop.

Don't leave more of a trace than necessary, she thinks. *And be quiet about it too.*

Spectra considers her options. She can try to climb without the use of her feet. She's never done that before. She knows from gym class that she can hold herself up by squeezing her legs on a rope, but this drain pipe is harder and it's against the wall. If she removes her boots, she'll be able to use her feet and wedge herself against the siding, like she normally does. It sounds like the quieter option too. She decides that it's the correct choice.

She backs up into the grass and sits down. She unties and pulls off her boots. Her socks need to go too, so she removes them as well. With her feet free, she wiggles her toes. They are painted in a rainbow of fall colors, each toe with its own hue of October foliage.

Spectra stands back up and reassesses her situation.

She knows she only has one chance to get this right. It seems impossible. Her eyes dart around in planning. She shuts her eyelids and envisions the jump, just like Mikaela Shiffrin envisions her ski runs. *If it worked on the sled, why not on the house?* she thinks.

The air is crisp and wet.

Spectra opens her eyes.

With a final breath, she darts toward the siding. She leaps over the mud. Her left foot pushes off against the left side wall, redirecting her angle. She grabs onto the drain pipe with her left hand and extends her right foot out toward the right side-wall. The big toe on her left foot accidentally stubs against the wall adjacent to the pipe, creating a soft thud. The ball of her right foot lands firmly on the side-wall and she extends her right palm to form another point of tension.

She stops moving.

She's on the wall.

The mud is safely below her.

Spectra pauses to listen for movement inside. If her parents heard the thud of her left foot against the siding, they will check it out. Especially Hugh. He is generally curious about strange noises.

She doesn't hear any commotion.

With slow, deliberate movements, she raises her left hand and grabs higher on the pipe. Then she moves her right foot up the wall. She repeats, back and-forth, all the way up to the roofline on top of the first floor. From there, she reaches up over the gutter and inches herself to free her body weight and center of gravity enough to swing and roll up onto the roof. The gutter makes a creaking noise, but Spectra doesn't panic. She lightly steps her way over to her bedroom window and climbs in.

Spectra's room is a mess. There are copies of *O Magazine* on the floor. Books are off the bookshelf. There are two pairs of shoes near the closet, and a gold-painted pine cone has fallen off her desk. Spectra is a little disgusted with herself. It's her mess, and she knows that there's nobody to blame but herself. She decides she'll tidy her room a little bit now and then clean her room properly as soon as she's done saving the world. It will make her feel good to do that for herself.

Somebody is walking around downstairs. Spectra squints, which magically focuses her hearing.

If you live with people, you learn to identify them in many ways. Ruby's steps, her gait, are distinct from Hugh's or Liam's. The steps that Spectra hears belong to her mother, Ruby.

Spectra picks up a stack of books from the middle of the room and sets it off to the side. It's a stack of the books Ruby recommended to Spectra. It was also a bunch of books Spectra didn't like.

Ruby keeps giving her these books to try to make a point. She wants her own emotional suffering to be validated. She wants even more for the counterpoints to be invalidated. They all seem to feature some poorly written drivel about a bleak modern world and nobody taking action to fix it. There are no ninjas in Ruby's stories. No Wizards.

Spectra's favorite book growing up was *The Very Persistent Gappers of Frip*. She loved the way Capable acted and solved problems, even though she wasn't a wizard. As Spectra grew older, she fell in love with the story of *Matilda*. Then Spectra found *Harry Potter* and never looked back.

For stories, the medium can be the message. People generally don't care about Alexander Hamilton, but they can't wait to see Lin-Manuel Miranda rap about him. In the books that her mother feeds her, Spectra largely agrees with the complaints levied, but she can't stand the actual stories. And because Spectra has even the tiniest disagreement, Ruby gets abrasive, and Spectra rebels in her reading choices.

Spectra looks at the pile of books from her mother again. She feels disgusted.

There's a spot near the far wall that looks perfect for books like that.

Spectra is finishing up with moving the books out of the way when she hears Ruby call from downstairs.

"Spectra, dear, would you like any lunch?"

23

Ruby's voice reverberates in Spectra's bedroom as the situation sinks in.

Oh no, Spectra thinks.

People often talk about the fight or flight response to shocking and dangerous situations. They are missing one response. It's actually the fight or flight or freeze response, and Spectra is firmly in the third camp.

"Spectra? Are you hungry?"

Spectra's mind races through the situation. *How bad is this?*

There are two courses of action she could take. She could respond or stay silent. If she stays silent, Ruby might think Spectra isn't in her room. Conveniently, Spectra *is* in her room right now. So, if she responds, it will seem like she never snuck out. But Spectra knows that she can't be seen. Her legs are all cut up, and it would be a dead giveaway that she has been outside. She decides on a plan of action.

"I'm not really hungry, Mom. I've got a granola bar and an apple, and I had some yogurt earlier."

There's a pause before Ruby speaks again.

"What are you doing up there?" she asks.

The neurons in Spectra's brain start firing, making connections between personality traits, conversation skills, hobbies, and learned lessons. She knows that views are largely shaped by personal experiences and that if you want to persuade somebody, you need to connect first. She knows that "being informed" can mean "in agreement with" in the right context and that "discussing important issues" can mean "people need to agree with me." Ruby wants to hear that she's right. Everybody loves confirmation.

"I'm reading that book you gave to me," Spectra says. "It's riveting! I can't wait to discuss it at school with my friends."

It's a good answer for many reasons, but Spectra is the most pleased that it provides cover for her bedroom to remain silent as she sneaks back out the window. She feels like Gwen Ifill with her quick thinking. Spectra considers Gwen to have been a ninja of conversation.

"Oh, I loved that book," Ruby says. "It was devastating."

"Absolutely!" Spectra throws up a little bit in her mouth.

"Let me know if you get hungry or if you need anything."

Crisis averted.

Spectra lets out a mighty sigh.

There's a pivot in the situation.

Spectra needs Liam to join the mission to remove the blast tomato. She can hear him through the wall, playing video games. It's a relief. She didn't know if he would still be out of the house.

He might still be mad at me, she thinks.

If you live with somebody, you learn how they act and how they react to different situations. Within a family, this becomes second nature. Spectra anticipates Liam's reactions. She treats it like a verbal Stackelberg game, if there were such a thing. Spectra decides that there is such a thing now.

She thinks back to a strategy she used earlier in the summer. Liam had caught seven grasshoppers and put them all in a shoebox. He topped it with a pane of glass so that he could peer in. Spectra was worried that the grasshoppers couldn't breathe, but she knew that Liam wasn't concerned. It was a boy thing. He was always squishing bugs and incinerating ants with a magnifying glass. He didn't care about the lives of insects. Spectra also knew that Liam wouldn't believe her if she told him that they wouldn't jump out if he removed the glass. It sounded like a trap. Instead, she convinced him that the fun was in catching the grasshoppers, not in holding them. She told him that it was boring to just keep them in a box. "Boring" and "fun" are emotions that a ten-year-old boy responds to.

They went out to the yard with the shoebox and set it down in the grass. To Spectra's dismay, when Liam removed the glass lid, only one grasshopper jumped out. The other ones refused to jump. They either looked at Liam like he was a god, or simply feared they might hit their heads by jumping. Spectra admired the one grasshopper that jumped as much as she was disgusted with the six that refused. Because Liam was thinking about catching the grasshoppers again, he was disappointed as well. He dumped the box over and encouraged them to hop away. He still wanted to prove that he was better than they were, that his hands were faster than their legs.

When the grasshoppers started hopping away, Spectra put on an act.

"Was that a frog I just heard?" she said.

Liam perked up. To him, frogs were like grasshoppers that were worth more imaginary points. All his attention was diverted to trying to hear the *ribbit* of the frog.

This was the strategy that Spectra planned on using again. She knew that Liam wouldn't care that the world was about to go dark forever even though it is really super important that it doesn't, but he does care about the opportunity to have fun. She would talk about the fun stuff.

When Spectra knocks on his door, he, Liam, neon-clad and energetic, swings the door open wildly. His eyes meet hers like a laser.

"Could I come in, please?" Spectra asks.

Liam turns back toward his TV and lets her enter. He's playing *Minecraft*.

Liam is such a juvenile boy, she thinks when she sees the Logan Paul and *Rick and Morty* posters on the wall. *Why can't he watch something good, like Yolanda Gampp or Lindsay Ellis?*

His room is even more of a mess than Spectra's is. She moves some dirty laundry off the bed and sits down.

"I'm sorry about earlier," she says. "And thank you for not telling Mom and Dad that I was out of the house."

Liam stares back at her like his face is carved in Carrara marble.

"I want to make it up to you," Spectra continues. "I want you to join me on my adventure, and it is going to involve magic, and I think you get to crawl through this gross squishy hole and get all dirty."

She can tell that he's considering the offer, but he remains silent as a power play. As long as Spectra is the one talking, she's the one making the deal.

Spectra gives her brother her best puppy dog eyes.

"Please," she says.

Having tried self-sufficiency
Knowing that it's not enough
With humble hope that you agree
My tongue tries to do the tough

The task at hand was just too much

For one person all alone
Needing hands and tools and such
When I ventured the unknown

Together we could form a team
Analyze with both our smarts
A stunningly creative scheme
Beyond the sum of our parts

I tried to clear the fog myself
Through the forest, down the way,
And now I come to you for help
On my knees of pleas today

24

Liam decides that an afternoon spent with his sister is better than an afternoon playing *Minecraft* by himself, no matter how upset he is at her. And, for that, Liam is over the chestnut tree incident. Boys tend to have short memories and shorter grudges when it comes to their siblings. They are so used to bickering and fighting that any individual misdeed gets slotted into the memory category of "competitive games." Even the particularly malicious becomes colored as *all in good fun* unless the perpetrator never makes an attempt to reconnect with the victim. This is the line that boys draw between bullying and pecking order pranks. Spectra, having apologized and offered an adventure, has shown clear *buddyness* and thus proven that the chestnut tree incident wasn't bullying.

Liam is eager to help. He puts on his shoes and shuts off the game.

"Is there really going to be magic?" asks Liam.

"Yeah! I found the Magic Sled of Nir," Spectra says in excitement.

"Awesome! Can I play with it?"

"I think it would be best if I play with the magic sled and you crawl in the yucky hole."

Liam considers the offer. "How yucky?"

"You might have to cut the hole yourself."

"Gross!" Liam is disgusted and delighted.

"It's a dirty job of a scope that Mike Rowe would appreciate," says Spectra.

Liam becomes animated. Spectra motions with a finger to her lips that they need to be quiet while they are still in the house.

Spectra climbs out her window onto the roof again. The roofing is hard against her bare feet. Liam follows her out the window and then Spectra reinstalls the screen.

"Don't be scared," Spectra says.

Liam puffs up his chest and, in a voice too loud, retorts, "I'm not scared!"

Spectra points out the drain pipe and explains how they get down. She goes first. At the bottom, she drops directly into the mud and splashes grime up and down her legs. She wipes off as much as she can with her hands, but it mostly just smears into her skin.

Liam follows her down, but his technique is amateurish. He's a ninja noob. Both Morris siblings breathe easier when Liam's shoes hit the mud.

Spectra motions to Liam that he needs to wait a minute, walks over to her shoes and socks, sits down in the grass, and starts cleaning her feet the best she can.

"Where are we going, Sis?"

"We're going to go on an adventure with the doctors. We need to go to the Toth Medical Center first."

"Dr. Ophelia, the Morris kids are here," Dr. Molly shouts to the back room.

"Good, good, good," Dr. Thelma says, as she rushes in. "I've got a backpack full of tools and Dr. Ophelia is just making last-minute arrangements and finishing up charting."

"This is my brother, Liam," Spectra says, in

introduction.

"Nice to meet you, Liam," says Dr. Molly.

"You too," says Liam.

As introductions continue, the conversation turns to school, as if that were the only thing going on in a child's life. One panel of lights is shut off in the back of the building. Dr. Thelma asks if Liam is playing any sports. There's a second panel of lights, this one closer to the front, and it too is shut off. Dr. Molly asks if Spectra and Liam have their parents' permission to go on such a dangerous mission. Spectra gives a non-answer and Dr. Molly accepts it. A third panel of lights is shut off in the room adjacent to the waiting room. Dr. Thelma asks if Liam is scared of the task at hand. The door opens, and Dr. Ophelia enters the waiting room.

"Let's go," she says.

Dr. Ophelia waits for everybody to exit the building, then shuts off the last lights in the building.

They pass Hart Hardware on their way to Fourier Woods. It seems like one of the few buildings in town that is happy to be open.

"Liam, did you beat *Minecraft* today?" Spectra asks.

This is normally the kind of question that irks Liam, but he goes along with it. "I finished building a space station, and I'm going to build a spaceship and launch it."

"*Minecraft* lets you go into orbit?" asks Spectra.

Liam had seen a YouTube video of a spaceship launching into orbit and has wanted to try it ever since. One of the brilliant things about growing up in the modern world is that kids can search for anything they want and there's probably a video of somebody walking through the process, step-by-step. Spectra uses the Khan Academy videos to help with her homework and Liam uses *Minecraft* videos to help him build spaceships.

Before he can speak, Dr. Ophelia interrupts. "Do you want to be an astronaut when you grow up, Liam?"

"That'd be so lit!" Liam says.

Spectra's question gets ignored. She isn't a fan of adults ignoring her questions like they aren't worthy of answering.

"Lit?" asks Dr. Ophelia.

"Yeah. Straight fire," Liam says.

"Well, that's very admirable," says Dr. Molly.

"You are going to have to study really hard if you want to be something cool like an astronaut," Dr. Thelma adds. "How's school going?"

Liam is struggling outside of math and P.E. He's embarrassed that Mason did better on the spelling test the previous week.

"Liam is killing it in math," Spectra says.

"That's very... lit," says Dr. Thelma with a smile.

"It is lit up with a bonfire," adds Dr. Ophelia.

Dr. Molly cringes and interjects, "Keep it 100, Liam."

"I'm going to meet aliens," Liam says, "and I'm going to explore other planets like in Kerbal."

Dr. Ophelia is becoming more confused. She thinks kids have a whole different language today based on memes, which she just learned about. She worries about the future of language. She redirects that conversation, hoping not to become more exposed and disconnected with her youth. "And what about you, Spectra?" Dr. Ophelia asks. "What are you going to be when you grow up?"

Spectra smiles. "I'm going to be a ninja when I grow up."

Dr. Ophelia brings her hand to the back of her neck.

"Or a wizard. I haven't decided yet," Spectra adds.

"That's an interesting career path," Dr. Molly says.

"I like getting out into the world," Spectra says, "like we're doing right now. I like adventures. I like hiking trails, not treadmills."

"You have a wonderful wanderlust for life, Spectra," Dr. Molly says.

"It seems like I wouldn't have to worry about treadmills if I got a job as a ninja," Spectra says.

Dr. Ophelia looks at Dr. Thelma in confusion.

"Or a wizard," Spectra adds.

The surroundings become quiet as they leave the town limits.

Dr. Thelma starts discussing a team that she is getting pulled into at work when Dr. Molly suggests that they come up with a name for the five of them.

"The Astronauts!" says Liam.

The enthusiasm of a kid getting to name something is one of the purest pleasures in life.

"What a wonderful name," says Dr. Molly.

"Do you have any ideas, Spectra," asks Dr. Thelma, wanting to make sure that Spectra also gets a chance to come up with a name before the team makes a decision.

Spectra thinks about it for a moment. Because she sees herself as a ninja, she logically sees the team as a group of ninjas. Her favorite movie is about ninjas, or actually *wuxia*, which is like a Chinese equivalent. She loves *House of Flying Daggers* because Xiao Mei fights to destroy a society that doesn't treat her as she deserves. She uses martial arts and a heavy dose of sly intelligence to trick her oppressors and trap them in their own miscalculations. Mei doesn't complain, she fixes the problem.

"The House of Gashing Scalpels," she suggests.

The name comes off more gruesome than she wanted. She picked the wrong adjective, but now she won't be able to take it back.

"Oh my," says Dr. Ophelia.

"That's a little, much, don't you think?" asks Dr. Thelma.

"Yeah, sorry. The House of Gliding Scalpels?" Spectra suggests.

The original suggestion gets seared in everybody's minds, and they have trouble even hearing the revised idea.

"The Astronauts of Gashing Scalpels!" says Liam.

"Very creati—" says. Dr. Molly.

"How about something less… vivid?" suggests Dr. Ophelia.

"The cryo arterial photogenesis angiography team," says Dr. Molly, mocking Dr. Ophelia's insistence on professionalism when asking children to name something.

"What?" says Liam.

"It does have a nice ring to it," says Dr. Ophelia.

"Or, what about 'the children and physicians action team?'" suggests Dr. Molly.

"You know—" says Dr. Thelma in thought.

"No, I liked your first one better," says Dr. Ophelia.

"You know," Dr. Thelma repeats, "we could just call it the CAPA Team for short."

Dr. Ophelia and Dr. Molly each thought it was an acronym for their own preferred suggestions. They both liked the sound of "CAPA Team" on their tongues.

"Wonderful," says Dr. Ophelia with a smile of victory. "CAPA Team it is!"

"Yeah, I can live with that," says Dr. Molly.

With animated excitement, Liam adds, "but like, 'The Astronaut CAPA Team of Gashing Scalpels!"

Spectra can't help but smile.

There's a mathematical concept called "inflection points." To be technical, they occur when a second derivative of a function is zero. A first derivative is zero at a peak or valley, the places where a graph changes direction and starts moving either up or down. The inflection point is between the peak and the valley and represents moving from the peaky part of the curve to the valley part of the curve. The peaky part of the curve is a concave shape and the valley part is a convex shape.

Constance Hunter, Chief Economist at the financial advisory firm KPMG, says that you have to look for the inflection points. Her skill is predicting the future.

According to her, inflection points are much harder to identify than peaks or valleys. Spectra, for example, knows when she reaches the top of a hill or when her sled went through the Gate of Splitsies at the bottom of a dell. Inflection points are a better-hidden signal among all the noise.

Dr. Ophelia knows that the world is getting darker. The fog was just the first phase of a downward concave slope. What Dr. Ophelia is trying to find, as they walk toward Fourier Woods, is an indication of an inflection point. If there's an inflection point, the darkness will get worse, but it will trough and then subside. If there's an inflection point, the concave portion of the darkness curve will save the village of Ivv, even if the mission does not. If there isn't an inflection point, the downward slope of darkness will only get steeper until there is no light left and Ivv becomes blind to the forest and the trees.

The CAPA Team crosses past the three green laurel trees in the patchy grass before entering Fourier Woods. Dr. Ophelia turns back and scans the horizon. There is no inflection point.

25

"I stashed it behind a tree," Spectra says. "I think it is just up at the top of the next hill."

"And you say it's magic?" asks Dr. Ophelia.

Spectra is used to having people, especially adults, question her. She knows this is especially true about outrageous claims, like saying that a sled is magic.

"I know when I took the Magic Sled of Nir through the Gate of Splitsies earlier, I became two people at the same time."

"And the Gate of Splitsies?" asks Dr. Thelma.

"It's all very complicated," Spectra says. "There was this book in the library, *The Smoke of the Sinister*, that covered everything. It's hard to explain."

"Yeah, you said that," Dr. Ophelia says.

"I want to play with it!" says Liam.

"This is Spectra's toy, Liam," Dr. Molly says. "We have a scalpel that you'll get to—"

"A scalpel is not a toy," adds Dr. Ophelia.

"You are going to have a very important job, Liam," Dr. Thelma says. "It might even be more fun than playing with the Magic Sled." Dr. Thelma winks at Spectra.

"Okay, wait here a second," Spectra says.

The Gate of Splitsies is directly ahead of the CAPA Team, but Spectra stops them just prior to cresting the hill so that she can check everything out without them looking. From the top of the hill, she confirms that the gate is still there. She turns and leaves the trail, taking large, intentional steps onto the areas that she can see the ground. The Magic Sled of Nir is right where she left it, behind the biggest mockernut hickory she can see.

Spectra grabs the sled and returns to the trail.

"Here it is!" she says, triumphantly.

The reaction from the rest of the CAPA Team is more muted than Spectra expects. They see the sled as just a sled. Spectra feels like this was her big reveal, but it's the magic part that her audience is waiting for.

"Cool," Liam says in a sarcastic tone.

"This is the Magic Sled of Nir," Spectra says, thinking that she wasn't clear enough.

"That's really nice, Spectra," Dr. Molly says. "It's a wonderful looking sled."

Dr. Thelma looks at Dr. Ophelia. The look she gives is one of hesitation. Without saying anything, it's clear from just her facial expression that Dr. Thelma thinks they have been duped. They were led out into a forest by a girl that believes in magic, and it was a gullible waste of time. Dr. Ophelia returns the worried gaze.

"The Gate of Splitsies is just past this hill," Spectra says.

Spectra starts walking to the crest of the trail. She doesn't notice that behind her back, only Dr. Molly is following her, and she silently shrugs her shoulders toward the other doctors. Liam sits down on the trail, right in the dirt. He makes just enough noise doing so that it catches Spectra's attention. She turns around and sees the CAPA Team not even going through the motions for her.

"Please, just trust me you guys," Spectra says.

Dr. Molly squishes her forehead into her nose to give

Dr. Ophelia a threatening stare.

"Come on, Liam," Dr. Ophelia says, extending a hand to help him back up.

Liam grunts in disapproval but grabs her hand and returns to his feet. The entire CAPA Team walks to the crest of the hill.

"There," Spectra points.

The unmistakable hand of humanity sits at the trough of the dell: a smooth silver monument to our control over the world around us.

"Would you look at that," Dr. Thelma says to Dr. Ophelia.

Dr. Ophelia doesn't respond. Her lips purse and her eyes narrow.

"It's quite magnificent," says Dr. Molly.

"Straight fire!" says Liam.

"Isn't it?" says Spectra.

Spectra isn't sure if the sled will be magic twice. It isn't something that she mulled over when she recombined earlier, but now that she is relying on a second round of efficacy, she realizes that it is something she should have considered. Instead of making a fuss about it or expressing the uncertainty that she harbors, Spectra decides to act confidently and assume that it will work a second time.

The rest of CAPA Team watches silently as Spectra sets down her sled. Dr. Ophelia shoots a skeptical glance at the dirt underneath the steel runners. She remains silent.

Without saying anything, Spectra lines up the sled and prepares for the run. She looks over the detritus and the tracks from earlier in the day. It looks clean. She turns over her shoulder and looks straight at Liam. She smirks and then turns back without saying anything. She pushes off and starts roaring down the slope.

26

"Whoa!" Liam yells as he runs down the hill toward the Gate of Splitsies.

Both Spectras are dusting themselves off. They are doing it mostly for show.

"There's two of you!" Liam says.

"Yep," both Spectras say in unison.

The doctors aren't far behind Liam. Dr. Ophelia has a baffled look on her face. She walks through the gate and isn't split in two.

"That really is a magic sled!" says Dr. Molly.

Dr. Thelma comes around to get a look directly in Snick's eyes. She starts examining her as if Snick were a patient. "Can we check pressure?"

"I'm fine, we're both fine," both Spectras say, throwing their hands in downward motion.

This is the first time that Spectra has really heard her voice come out of two mouths at once. It is jarring and unexpected even though it is entirely expected. It creeps her out a little bit.

"Can I try? Can I try?" Liam says. He wants a second copy of himself.

"They both look good," says Dr. Thelma. "Can you

please open your tongues and say 'ahhhh'?"

"Stop pestering her, Dr. Thelma," Dr. Molly says. "She says—they say they are alright. Let's get back to our task at hand."

"But can I ride the sled first?" asks Liam.

"You'll get your turn to do something cool soon enough, Liam," says Dr. Ophelia. "This was Spectra's thing. You need to let her have it."

Mac does her best not to smile. She doesn't want to look like she is gloating. She doesn't want Liam to feel left out. She tries not to smile, but a tiny upward curve starts on one side.

Both Spectras hike up the other side of the dell and find a good spot for the Magic Sleds of Nir just off the trail behind large tree trunks. The rest of the CAPA Team are reading the poem about the two paths. Snick and Mac walk back down.

"This is Snickerdoodle Hufflepuff," but Snick and Mac point to the left, "and this is Macaroon Ravenclaw," they both point to the right. Realizing the issue of both Spectras pointing the same direction, they add, "Snick on your left, Mac on your right."

"Nice to meet you, Snick and Mac," Dr. Molly says.

"Those are stupid names," Liam says.

"Well, I like them," Dr. Molly says.

"As do I—we," Snick and Mac say.

"What now?" Dr. Thelma asks.

The Spectras explain that Snick will walk the path toward Refarm and Mac will walk down the path toward Fomacula. They are still having trouble with pointing, but they indicate that everybody else will come with Mac, toward Fomacula.

The doctors are convinced to start hiking again before they calm down. Liam doesn't need convincing. He's amped up and ready to go.

Dr. Ophelia looks over her shoulder as she crests the

other side of the dell to get a final look at Snick, walking away in a different direction.

"Hear that?" Mac asks.

"Is that an accordion?" asks Dr. Thelma.

"Don't tell me," says Dr. Molly. "I can get it."

The song sounds familiar to all of them, but it takes until the chorus for any of them to recognize the song. They all figure it out on the exact same note.

"A-ha!" exclaims Dr. Molly. "*99 Red Balloons!*"

"Set them free at the break of dawn, 'til one-by-one they were gone," Dr. Thelma sings.

The CAPA Team approaches Negelem and his song gets louder.

"Unpopular opinion, but I prefer the Goldfinger version," says Dr. Molly.

"That's hokum," says Dr. Thelma. "There's only one version of Luftballoons. Nena singing in a jacket with smoke rising from the ground in the background."

"You were just singing the English version," Dr. Molly says. "What about the German version?"

"Just—" says Dr. Thelma.

"And didn't Nena redo it like 20 years later?"

"It's okay for you two to have different preferences," says Dr. Ophelia. "There doesn't have to be a correct answer."

"See, that's what I'm saying," says Dr. Molly. "I *prefer* the Goldfinger version—"

"Uh-huh," says Dr. Thelma.

"Because it is objectively better."

Mac isn't familiar with Goldfinger, but she thinks, *this would make a good song for Lindsey Stirling.*

The music stops.

"Hey Mac," Negelem says.

"Hi Negelem," Mac says. "This is my brother, Liam," she points, "and these doctors are with me too. We're a team. We call ourselves The House of Gliding Scalpels."

"Gashing," Liam corrects.

"You named your hiking crew?" Negelem asks. "I can dig it."

"The Astronauts of Gashing Scalpels," Liam says.

"We're just the CAPA Team for now," says Dr. Ophelia.

There's an awkward standoff. Mac breaks the silence. "We're going to go back to Fomacula. Turns out there's something wrong there. The whole world is in danger."

This catches Poselem's attention and he moves to his brother's side.

"It's very important," says Liam.

"Huh," says Poselem.

"And dangerous," Liam adds.

"Oh yeah," says Poselem.

"And I'm going to use a scalpel and get all mucky," Liam says.

"It's very admirable," Dr. Molly says, putting a hand on Liam's shoulder.

"It's nice to see you boys again," Mac says. "But we really should be on our way, so we have enough time to save the world before dinner."

"Oh," says Poselem.

Mac turns to Dr. Ophelia. "It's really important that we get back by dinner time."

"We'll see what we can do," Dr. Ophelia says.

"I guess, see you soon," Negelem says.

"Yep," Mac says with a wave. "Bye boys."

27

"I think it moved," Mac says.

She is staring at the large blank golden sign in front of her in the path toward Fomacula.

Brooke Lampley is the Vice Chairman of the Fine Arts division at Sotheby's, the auction house. She is tasked with valuing pieces of art that have no equivalent. She must verify the authenticity and decide how much the market would value a new piece. Her ability to accurately identify and classify works of art depends on a trained eye. She has seen thousands of equivalent works, so she can instantly get a feel for any given new one. Having seen previous works, she has something to compare to when assessing authenticity.

If Mac was assessing the sign as it is versus how it was previously, she would be using the same type of trained eye that Brooke Lampley uses to assess the authenticity of magnificent paintings. Mac doesn't have the same level of training yet for the golden sign in front of her, but this is the third time she has seen it. Her ability to see the change in that sign is predicated on her trained eye noticing the change from the previous two times she has seen it. Mac definitely thinks the sign has moved.

"How did it move?" Dr. Thelma asks.

"Like, I think it was in the same spot before, but…" Mac is struggling to describe the change. "It just feels off. It would be a small change, I guess, but it seems like a different angle or something."

"Why would it be at a different angle?" Dr. Thelma asks.

"And how can you tell?" asks Dr. Ophelia.

Most compressed memory formats are similar. JPEG compression, for example, is similar to MP3 compression, and both are similar to old VHS tapes. They work by only identifying change. If a series of red bricks in a retaining wall all have the same hue, but there's one particular one that is a darker shade of red, and then every brick beyond that point continues to be the darker shade, and two things are known. First, there was a point where something switched. Maybe the supplier or the pile of bricks changed, but there was unquestionably a specific point of change. And second, the brick layer didn't do a good job.

Compression algorithms, like JPEG and MP3, read data like Mac would see the bricks in the wall. She doesn't examine each brick individually for color; she notes that the first seventeen are red and the next twenty-five are dark red. There's one piece of information to note and remember: the change.

Mac has reduced the golden sign problem down to a single conclusion. It has changed. It is different than it was before. If Mac was the Brooke Lampley of blank golden signs, she would be able to articulate the way in which it changed. Unfortunately, Mac isn't the Brooke Lampley of blank golden signs; she's just a brick counter that happened upon a change. She can identify only the most basic piece of information about the sign.

"Last time I came down this path, I think it was more at *this angle*," Mac motions with her entire arm. "I know it doesn't make any sense, but I'm pretty sure it moved."

Normally, when Mac is hiking, she passes the same people twice. She might pass them several times. She takes a break in the shade to get some water and they pass her again. Then, if she is the faster hiker, she passes them on the trail.

Mac is expecting to see the triplets again. Annabel and Brianna aren't between the golden signs anymore, and Mac concludes that Joanna is gone as well.

Hiking is wonderful. Being out in nature, out in the quiet, peaceful forest allows a mind to wander. It allows for contemplation about the big questions. When Annabel had her phone in her face, Mac couldn't help but pity her. Annabel can't handle boredom. Mac, or Spectra, for that matter, loves boredom. Not in the moment, of course, but after the fact, as she becomes riveted by her own mind-wandering. Those who travel and want to travel are said to have wanderlust. Spectra needs boredom; she needs the quiet forest to satiate her mental wanderlust. Her mind is wandering and pondering how hiking is like a certain trip she took to the pool.

One time when Spectra went swimming, she noticed some interesting things. Prior to jumping in, when she looked in a mirror she saw herself. That was reflection. She went out to a table by the pool and set her water bottle down. Her water bottle had a straw in it. As Spectra drank the water, she noticed that the straw looked like it was bending. That was refraction. When Spectra got into the pool and dove under the surface, she looked up and was amazed. The surface of the water looked bright right above her but looked endless as it stretched further out.

Spectra got curious. She decided to run a scientific experiment. She wanted to know what happened if she brought a light under the water. When swimming previously, the light was always above the surface, out in the air. *There must be a way to shine from below*, she thought.

She found a Ziploc bag and put a laser pointer inside. When she dove in, she had a light that she could test out under the surface. As she pointed up through the bright area above her head, she saw a spot up on the ceiling, way above the surface. When she pointed at the area of the surface that looked like endless water, she noticed that it reflected back into the pool. Spectra ran another experiment. She held the laser pointer in the Ziploc bag up above her head, near the surface, but still below, at a shallow angle. It was still hitting the part above her that looked bright, but the laser light reflected back into the water.

Later, she wanted to understand what was going on, so she went to the library. She found a book that talked about Total Internal Reflection. As it turns out, as Spectra made the angle of the laser pointer shallower and shallower, it went from refracting to reflecting at what was referred to as the critical angle. Beyond that critical angle, the laser light reached Total Internal Reflection, and bounced back into the pool.

As Mac is hiking, she considers that she could exit the trail, but it would really only work if she exited at a deep enough angle. If she tried to slowly enter the overgrowth and shrubbery, it would be too difficult. The trail and the forest form a surface boundary and Mac may hike on the edge, but she always returns to center core of the path. She has reached Hiking Trail Reflection, just like her laser pointer in the pool.

28

The CAPA Team passes the second golden sign of unknown provenance. It has also moved, but Mac doesn't worry about making a fuss. She understands that the doctors aren't interested in the signs.

Liam puts his arms straight out and starts making airplane noises. Mac laughs at her silly little brother.

"Who brought an airplane with us?" Dr. Molly asks.

"I'm a spaceship," says Liam.

"Bless your heart," says Dr. Ophelia.

"I think if you're in space, your spaceship doesn't make sound," says Dr. Thelma. "The sound comes from the air in our atmosphere."

Liam stops for a second, thinks about what Dr. Thelma said, and then continues flying and sputtering his mouth for sound effects. "My spaceship makes noise."

"Is that how your spaceship in *Minecraft* sounds, Liam?" asks Dr. Thelma.

Liam sputters harder.

"That's quite the good spaceship, Liam," Mac says.

Liam makes a landing motion and jumps on the ground. His sound effects imply an explosion, but it's clear by his body language that the spaceship is fine.

"Did you land on an alien planet?" asks Dr. Molly.

Liam thinks about the prospect. He decides that would be fun. "Yes," he says. There's a pause of thought, then he asks, "Do spaceships ever get stuck on alien planets?"

The question catches everybody off guard. Dr. Ophelia takes it and says, "We haven't yet."

Liam presses the issue. "What would happen if they did get stuck?"

"You would probably need to send another spaceship out there to help it," says Dr. Molly.

"What kind of spaceship?" Liam asks.

"Well," Dr. Molly says, "I suppose it would be kind of like a tugboat. A tugboat in space."

"Are there spaceboats too?" Liam asks.

"Maybe you could build a spacetugboat in *Minecraft*, Liam," Mac suggests. "You could be the very first kid to ever make a spacetugboat."

"Wait," Liam says. He's thinking about implementing Mac's suggestion. "What's the difference between a ship and a boat?"

"I think it is about the size," says Dr. Thelma.

"Maybe something to do with the sails?" posits Dr. Molly.

"A spacetugboat can get your spaceship off the planet where it's stuck," Mac says, "but I think you still need the spaceship to get back home."

Liam processes the answers and then starts making what is assumed to be tugboat sounds. Then he makes a rocket launch sound and starts flying with his arms again.

"This is the Rare Bee Expanse," Mac says, pointing just ahead.

"The what?" asks Dr. Ophelia.

"You know," Mac says, "for helping out with rare bees."

"But I don't like bees!" Liam wails.

"It'll be okay, Liam," Mac says. "These are nice bees.

They won't sting you."

Mac didn't know whether or not her statement was true, but she knew that she needed Liam to think that it's true in order to enter the Rare Bee Expanse.

"We have seen some strange things today, but I think this might be the strangest," says Dr. Ophelia.

"Oh, it's not that bad," says Dr. Thelma.

Everybody has secret worries inside them. Right now, Liam is worried about the bees. It isn't much of a secret anymore, but he is also worried about what the doctors think of him now that they know he's afraid of bees. The doctors don't care. They have their own worries.

Dr. Ophelia grew up in a strict environment. She grew up by the book, and in her early life, there was no question which book that was. Having seen Spectra split into two, Dr. Ophelia has an unvoiced moral objection to *The Smoke of the Sinister* and any tricks it may be playing with the world. The only reason she hasn't spoken out about her worry is that she is putting the mission first.

Dr. Thelma is still thinking like the doctor she is. She wants to run some tests on Mac to make sure that she's alright. Dr. Thelma worries that being split into two is going to have some long-term negative consequences to Mac's health.

Dr. Molly is concerned about the other two doctors. They aren't as interested in listening to Mac as she is, and it may ruin the plan to remove the blast tomato. Dr. Molly wants everybody to be on the same page but doesn't know how to suggest a reconciliation without highlighting the disconnect, thus potentially causing an argument.

Mac worries about getting home by dinnertime. She needs to sneak back into the house to prevent being seen, and if they aren't back by dinner, there's no way that will happen.

"How big is he expanse?" asks Liam.

"Not too long," Mac says. "Maybe a 20-minute walk."

"Twenty minutes!" Liam says.

"It will be nice," Mac says. "There's wonderful flowers in a whole bunch of different colors and the bees are nice too."

Liam is miserable, so to him, the hiking seems like it is taking forever.

"I don't want to," Liam says.

The doctors look at each other. They remain silent and let Mac diffuse the situation.

Different people find different things difficult. For Liam, walking through an expanse of buzzing stingers is not only fear-inducing, it is difficult. Mac isn't struggling with the Rare Bee Expanse, so it doesn't seem like something worth getting worked up over, and she has a hard time fully empathizing with Liam's emotional anguish.

"Harry Potter was locked in under a staircase and he didn't complain," Mac says. "You get to go on an adventure outside in nature. Maybe you should act more like Harry Potter, Liam."

The comment doesn't go over well. Liam is fuming. Fortunately, he bottles it up and they walk into the Rare Bee Expanse.

Halfway through the Rare Bee Expanse, Liam gets stung by a bee.

"Owwww!!!!" Liam wails.

Dr. Molly is the first to Liam.

"What happened?" she asks.

"I was stung," Liam says.

Liam is grabbing his left arm. Dr. Molly lifts his right hand from the spot where he was stung. There's a stinger at the center of a red mound.

Mac feels guilty. She had just told Liam that everything would be alright.

Dr. Thelma searches in her bag. She pulls out tweezers and an alcohol swab and hands them to Dr. Molly.

Dr. Molly removes the stinger with the tweezers. She

then swabs down the hole where the stinger used to be. Liam starts to whimper at the pain of the alcohol. Dr. Thelma grabs a band-aid and puts it on the area of concern. She applies a cold pack to the wound.

Mac asks, "How are you doing, buddy?"

Liam says, "Okay," but it comes out more like a cry for help.

"You are going to be just fine, Liam," Dr. Molly says. "You are handling this so well."

The compliment boosts Liam's mood. As much as he hates the pain in his arm, he wants to be the kind of boy that *can* handle something like this well. He sniffles a few times and wipes his nose with the backside of his wrist.

"I'm doing good," Liam says to Mac, but the glare he gives her implies he feels betrayed.

"Are you sure?" asks Mac.

"Yes," he says. He turns to Dr. Molly and says, "Thank you."

"What should we do?" Mac asks. "Do we need to turn back and take you home?"

Liam looks deeply into Mac's eyes. She knows his answer.

29

Liam and the rest of the CAPA Team continue onward. They exit the Rare Bee Expanse and find the shining hole to enter Fomacula.

"Would you look at that," Dr. Ophelia says.

"Isn't it pretty?" says Dr. Molly.

The sun is at a much lower angle, so it doesn't directly fall through the hole in the fog, but blue sky is visible.

"It must be some sort of wind or air pressure from this hole," Dr. Ophelia says.

"I think this is the first time I've seen blue sky in months!" says Dr. Thelma.

Mac is awed by the sight, but not as much as the rest of her companions. She had already seen the hole, and the second time it feels like the magic is gone. Ruby always says, "do something once or do it all the time." She means that the first time is impressive, and only with consistency does the magic return. Through repeated experience, Mac might acquire the same trained eye for fog holes that Brooke Lampley has for art. At that point, she would really appreciate the beauty once again. On this second viewing however, she isn't in awe like the others are.

"Could we fall through the sky?" Liam asks.

"You can always fall through the sky, Liam," Dr. Molly says. "Fog won't stop you from falling."

"What is fog made of?" Liam asks.

"Tiny water droplets," says Dr. Molly. "They are suspended in the air when it is cold and wet enough. That's why you feel so damp."

Liam thinks about that for a few seconds. He decides that he understands what she means, and he nods his head in agreement.

"What happens now?" Dr. Thelma asks Dr. Ophelia.

"Well, I think we—" says Dr. Ophelia.

"We climb down," Mac interrupts. She points down into the hole. "That cave is Fomacula. That is where we need to go."

The philosopher Plato presented his famous allegory of the cave to explain the effect of education. He explained that a person who only saw the shadows in his cave from the outside world would be unable to comprehend the world beyond the cave. The way that Plato presents the allegory is as an intellectual silo. Plato presented philosophy as the method for overcoming the intellectual silos that we choose to bury ourselves in.

In the era of the internet, Plato's cave might have been presented as an echo chamber or a filtered news feed. Hugh Howey's novel *Wool* took the concept to the extreme and examined what life really would be like if we holed ourselves up in a literal silo. The revelation, for Plato and for Howey, was that people can't handle the reveal. If they realize they have had the world hidden from them, they revolt.

Mac is peering into a cave and has a different reaction. From the side of the normal world, discovering the small, hidden Fomacula, she doesn't feel as though she has been lied to. She feels as though there are still mysteries in the world, still magic to be found. She becomes hopeful in having discovered something beyond her understanding.

Mac doesn't get upset about the cave because it is a small discovery, while Plato's allegorical cave-dwellers find a huge world beyond their tiny cave. Mac's pleasure of discovery is inversely proportional to the amount of her knowledge that it upends. The world is scary when everything turns out to be a lie, but beautiful when a small mystery reveals secrets in doses. Babies cry as much as they do because the world is more than they can process. Travelers to exotic foreign countries book expensive, comfy hotels to avoid being bombarded by too much *new* at once. Dr. Ophelia sees the hole as more than she can comprehend. She has been around for many years and the things she has seen throughout the day continue to make her uneasy.

Mac also has the perspective of Snick to compare with. Her unique ability to analyze and contrast the two places at once allows her to be both at the cave and away from the cave at the same time. The magic ability to comprehend the interference of these two environments is beyond anything Plato had conceived of. She understands more than the either cave-dweller and the not-cave-dweller alone. In her super position, she understands the difference in the phase of each of those two perspectives. Mac doesn't realize it, but she sees details in the cave that the doctors don't see. She has hyper-precise resolution vision. She is seeing in ultra-high definition, while the doctors are stuck in standard definition.

Mac descends first into the cave. She is eager to complete the daring mission. The rest of the CAPA Team follows, but Dr. Ophelia lingers at the rim before accepting her fate. She is holding her tongue, keeping the team on task.

"It feels organic," Dr. Thelma says.

Dr. Molly bends down and touches the red net below her feet. The surface is cool and slimy. She pushes with her palm. It has some give and bounce.

"What is this place?" asks Liam.

"It's Fomacula," Mac says.

"Yeah, but *what* is this place?" Liam repeats.

"I suppose that's part of the question we must resolve," says Dr. Molly.

Liam starts bouncing on the surface like a trampoline.

"The membrane is some kind of epithelium," says Dr. Ophelia.

"More like an 'Epi-*weee*-Liam'," says Liam.

Mac is pleased to see that her brother is no longer bothered by the bee sting. Or, at least, he is distracted into a better mood.

"This place is truly magnificent," says Dr. Molly. "Did you see these red vias? They branch out like—"

"I know," Dr. Ophelia says.

"I noticed that too," Dr. Thelma says.

"It couldn't *actually* be? Could it?" asks Dr. Molly.

Mac is lost in the conversation. The doctors appear to know something that they aren't letting on. They are making a diagnosis and not telling her.

"What else did that book... what was it called, '*The Smoke of the Sinister*'; what did it say about Fomacula?" asks Dr. Thelma.

"I can't really remember," Mac says. "There was something about Dexter and removing the smoke."

"None of this makes sense," says Dr. Ophelia.

"And yet," says Dr. Molly, "It all kind of does."

"What is it? What's going on here?" asks Mac.

"When Dr. Thelma said it feels organic," says Dr. Molly, "what she was implying is that this red net surface below our feet is—we're inside something that's alive."

30

One of the major differences between Mac and the doctors is their depth of knowledge. The doctors have very deep knowledge in the medical field, but this is also a narrow focus. They have coherent thoughts that travel a long way before scattering. The world needs doctors. We need people that dedicate themselves to a single area of importance and focus so intensely on it, that they become experts. We especially need this in matters of life and death, as is true for doctors.

Mac is different, possibly because she is still so young. Mac, or Spectra rather, wants to be both a ninja and a wizard. She hasn't picked one career yet. She has a wider band of influence from school and society that allow her to spread out and try different hats in life. This broad perspective changes how she perceives the world as compared to the doctors. Spectra couldn't solve a medical issue like the doctors can, but she can try to approach problems as a wizard if approaching it as a ninja doesn't work. She is, as they say, a wizard of many trades, a ninja of even more.

Liam is even broader in focus than Spectra. He likes astronauts, but he isn't serious about trying to become one yet. He may babble incoherently about things he still knows very little about because he is still young enough that limiting his focus prematurely would darken possibilities before he gets the chance to explore them. Liam still needs to illuminate as many paths as he can. However, due to his spread of interests, he isn't particularly useful in any field. With time, as he matures and studies, he will limit his scope and excel at one particular thing, but for now he is a *Minecraft* builder of everything, astronaut of nothing.

The different perspectives are useful for different tasks. In the chamber of Fomacula, the doctors see what they know; they see biology. When you've got a scalpel, everything looks like an organism. Their assessment of Fomacula being alive could be correct, but it is a conclusion they were prepared to reach no matter what they found.

"You'll need this syringe," Dr. Ophelia says to Mac.

"And I'll go over there with it," asks Mac, pointing.

"Yes," says Dr. Ophelia. "And you will wait for my word."

"Got it," Mac says.

Dr. Ophelia turns to Liam and says, "Liam, I am going to use this scalpel to cut a hole at the base of the mound. You will need to crawl in and apply cryotherapy to the dysplasia."

"What's that?" Liam asks.

"A scalpel is a like a little doctor's knife," Dr. Ophelia says.

"No," says Liam. "What is the splay-shia?"

"She wants you to freeze off the blast tomato," Mac says.

Dr. Molly steps forward and states, "We are a team, Dr. Ophelia. Please keep the conversation on a level that Liam can understand. We all have important roles in this operation and we need to work as a single unit."

"Understood, Doctor," Dr. Ophelia says.

Dr. Molly is pleased with herself.

"Dr. Thelma," Dr. Ophelia continues, "will photocoag— will shine a really bright flashlight to ablate— to burn away tiny spots of the blast tomato."

Dr. Molly smiles.

"Dr. Molly," Dr. Ophelia says, "will need to pull back the red net to create the hole for Liam." She pauses to consider how to phrase her instructions. She looks at Dr. Molly and says, "You will need to swing that way, but be careful. If you sail too far, there might be a boom."

"Aye, Aye, Cap'n," Dr. Molly says, pleased with herself, "I be scannin' the main luff and holdin' me sheet."

Dr. Ophelia shoots Dr. Molly a serious look.

Mac wonders if Dr. Molly missed her true calling as a pirate. She isn't sure, however, why anybody would choose to be a doctor over the respected profession of sailing the seven seas. *Doctors don't even have ships*, she thinks.

There's an old Greek myth of Sisyphus. Sisyphus was like an ancient ninja king that got caught while trying to be sly. He was punished by the gods. Sisyphus was required to push a giant boulder up a steep hill. The boulder was heavy, and the task was arduous. When Sisyphus made it to the top of the hill, the gods rolled the boulder back to the bottom. He returned down the hill and started rolling the large rock back up the hill once again. This punishment went on for an eternity. Every time Sisyphus reached the top of the hill, the gods punished him again by making him repeat the task.

This is the second time Mac has journeyed to Fomacula, but it surely would be the last. When Dr. Ophelia was unable to find an inflection point in the fog, she determined that the CAPA team would only have one opportunity to remove the blast tomato. Spectra doesn't have eternity to complete her mission.

Removing the blast tomato is a delicate, coordinated

process. It is monumental in scope. If Sisyphus had to roll a boulder up a hill, Mac has to roll one up Mr. Everest. CAPA Team has come a long way on their journey, but the reality is that they have only just arrived at the start of their mission. All the critical work, the dangerous operation, is yet to come. Mac is pushing a boulder up Everest, but she's only yet reached Base Camp 1.

31

Mac grabs the syringe in her right hand. She walks over to her station, at the large red mound. She is separated from the rest of the CAPA Team, who all focus directly on the bulbous red blast tomato.

"Right here?" Mac asks.

"Yeah, that's perfect!" says Dr. Thelma.

Dr. Ophelia packed a varied set of tools for anything she thought they might need as well as anything that a traveling doctor should have on hand. The doctors carried a medical kit, an AED, chemicals for injection, and the specialized tools specific to removing a blast tomato. Dr. Thelma is given the laser system for photocoagulation, a spot ablation and destruction technique for the blast tomato using a high-intensity, focused beam.

"Can you see fine from there?" Dr. Thelma asks.

Mac is well-positioned on top of a volcano-like hill. There is a crater at the top, but she is stationed on the rim for the time being.

"Yeah!" Spectra says. "It's actually a great view from here."

Dr. Thelma turns on the laser. There's a pleasant shungggg sound, followed by a low hum of a large energy draw from a battery pack. She points it at the blast tomato and starts the ablation process.

Dr. Molly hands Liam a small probe. "This button will turn on the cryo— the freeze ray," she says. "Point it only at the blast tomato. If you hold down the button too long, it may start to get cold in between the layers and you are in danger of freezing your own hand. Only hold the button for a couple seconds."

"Thank you," Liam says, not knowing how else to respond.

Dr. Ophelia uses her scalpel to start cutting a slit where the mound meets the floor of the red net. She slashes in a single direction, left to right.

Dr. Molly uses a set of forceps to pinch the lip of the slit. She hoists herself up on top of the mound, laying on her stomach, and grabs the handles of the forceps. She pulls back, opening the slit as wide as it will go.

Liam peers into the slit. He sees flashes of light from Dr. Thelma's laser tool. It reminds him of a lightning storm, which doesn't make the crawlspace more appealing.

"Go for it, Liam!" Dr. Ophelia says.

He hesitates momentarily. He turns over his shoulder and looks at Mac. She gives him a thumbs up and then waves him forward. Liam turns back toward the slit at the intersection of the mound and the red net. He takes a breath and eases himself in.

"Now!" Dr. Ophelia shouts.

Mac jumps down from the rim of the red mound into the crater. Not only is the surface bright red, it is pulsing, up and down. Her hands are sweating from the heat, humidity, and the seriousness of the situation, but she keeps a firm grip on the syringe.

She looks at the very center of the crater, the spot she wants to stab, and then looks back at her syringe. Mac doesn't like needles. She doesn't even like being on the giving side of one. The power she harnesses doesn't make her feel stronger, it makes her feel vile. She centers her thoughts and lunges forward toward the center of the crater. Her right knee hits the ground and she braces her body with her left arm. She jabs the needle through the surface and lets out a loud warrior grunt.

She holds the syringe barrel firmly with her right hand and grabs the plunger flange on top with her left. She tries to push down, but she doesn't have the strength or leverage to make progress.

"This part, right here," Mac hears Dr. Ophelia call out to Liam in the distance.

Mac leaps forward and lands on the plunger flange with her chest. Her entire weight is suspended in the air by the syringe. Her right hand does nothing for stabilization with her weight suspended on the syringe rather than the ground. The syringe starts to tip, but the plunger is moving into the barrel. Liquid is flowing out into the red net.

She reaches her left hand out and braces herself. The syringe steadies. Mac is able to apply her weight more precisely in the direction she needs to. The plunger keeps diving deeper and deeper into the barrel of the syringe. It hits the bottom. All the fluid is in the underground red net below her.

Mac breathes.

She sits back and pulls the syringe from the surface. It feels light in her shaking hand.

"Yuck!" Mac hears Dr. Ophelia gasp. There's a sound of something of a mud-like consistency plopping onto the ground.

Life returns to Mac's arms. She is exhausted, but she is recovering from the exertion.

"You're doing great, Liam!" Dr. Molly says in encouragement.

Mac climbs back up to the rim of the crater. She peers out toward the blast tomato.

"Keep going, Liam," Dr. Ophelia says. "You're almost

there!"

Mac sees Liam underneath the surface of the blast tomato. She can see him with the freeze probe in his hand. She can see that he is lifeless.

"He's not breathing," Mac shouts.

"What do you mean?" asks Dr. Ophelia. "How could you even know that from way back there?"

"I can see him," Mac says. "I can see through the layers. There's so many layers, but I can see right through him."

"Breathing is too subtle to be seen from there, Spectra," Dr. Ophelia says to Mac.

"Maybe it is too subtle for you, but I can see the smallest details," Mac says.

Dr. Ophelia looks at Dr. Thelma. She doesn't believe Mac. To go after Liam would jeopardize the whole plan. They decide to take no action. They go back to cutting and ablating.

What are they doing? Mac thinks.

"Can't you see that he's not breathing!" Mac shouts.

The doctors continue with their plans, ignoring Mac's plea. They must not be able to see the lack of subtle movement of Liam's diaphragm deep underneath layers of organic tissue. They don't have the right tools for the job.

Liam is stuck. He isn't breathing.

Mac knows she must crawl into the blast tomato and save him.

Adele DeCruz, a research associate at the American Museum of Natural History, works on art restoration. She uses a laser ablation tool that she patented to remove layers of varnish that obstruct the beautiful original pigments on paintings. It is a delicate removal process and she must be incredibly precise. To ensure that she only removes the varnish, she images the paintings using a handheld Optical Coherence Tomography device. This allows her to see micron-level details beneath the surface of the painting. Her abilities go beyond simply being an expert; she has the right tools for the job.

Liam is like the brick-counter, not having any expertise, but able to determine the smallest, and most obvious, pieces of information. Doctors Ophelia, Thelma, and Molly just have their own expertise and training to help them process the situation. They are like Brooke Lampley, the Sotheby's art expert that can verify authenticity with only her own trained eyes. Spectra is like Adele DeCruz. She has more than just expertise, she has the right tool. She is an entire order of magnitude more perceptive and precise in her assessment.

Snick's vision in Refarm combines knowledge with Mac's in Fomacula, giving her the ability to determine the very smallest of details. This is how Mac knows that Liam isn't breathing, even from a distance. The doctors are missing the small details. The infinitesimal is perceivable with the duel perspective. When the problem is parallel to health, the doctors have the deep knowledge required. This particular problem isn't just about health though, it is a normal problem. The orthogonal direction of the situation means that Mac's wide band of interests give her the deeper understanding. Mac can see the layers beneath the surface, while the doctors only assess the epithelial layer. Only Mac can see Liam stuck underneath the blast tomato.

Mac has true knowledge of the situation. The Magic Sled of Nir makes all the difference, as does Optical Coherence Tomography for Adele DeCruz. The doctors think they see what's happening, but they can't. It isn't their fault, they just don't have the right tools. Their opinions are formed based on what they can perceive, which isn't enough. Mac is the only person that can save Liam. She must act on her knowledge and crawl into the blast tomato to save her brother.

She let him down when he fell from the chestnut tree. She let him down when they went through the Rare Bee Expanse. She gave him the thumbs-up about the blast tomato, and he once again trusted her. She can't let him down again. Her little brother's life is in danger.

Mac dashes toward the blast tomato to save Liam's life.

32

"What are you doing?" Dr. Ophelia says.

Mac doesn't pay attention. She crawls in underneath the blast tomato.

"Don't stop Liam," Dr. Ophelia says. "He is doing his job!"

Mac is surrounded by slime and guts of the organic red net. The weight from above is crushing. Dr. Molly is trying to open the hole as wide as she can, but it's too heavy.

Mac crawls between the layers, digging deeper. She reaches Liam's right foot. She tries to pull it, but he doesn't have the anchoring to pull him from the same slit that she is in. The more she pulls Liam out, the more she also pulls herself in. *For every action, there is an equal, but opposite reaction*, she thinks. She grabs the freeze probe from Liam's hand and points it above his head. She clicks the button. The blast tomato above him hardens, but it doesn't disappear. He is still being crushed by the blast tomato.

Up above, Dr. Thelma is trying to ablate the area above Mac and Liam, but she can't get close enough to their heads without risking ablating the kids.

"Swing," shouts Dr. Ophelia.

Dr. Molly jumps with the forceps in her hands and tries

to wrench the blast tomato out of the ground. She rips part of the side.

Dr. Ophelia continues to cut at the intersection of the bulbous structure and the ground. The scalpel is woefully inadequate for the job. She needs a machete. Physicians don't normally carry machetes.

Mac tries freezing more of the blast tomato above Liam. She forms a hardened shell. She sets the freeze probe to the side and does a pushup with all her arm strength to create a cavity for Liam to breath. It doesn't revive him. He lays lifeless next to her.

As Mac realizes that her plan isn't working, she decides she needs to reformulate a new plan. She pushes past Liam and turn around so that she can push him out, rather that pull him. Sweat is dripping down her face, mixing with the liquid spewing from the red net.

She wiggles as far as she can, but she is only able to manage a torso length before she hits a wall. With no further to crawl, she turns sideways. She inches around and with her back to the blast tomato and her chest facing Liam's head, she pushes on his shoulders.

Liam's body scrunches. His feet stay still, but his shoulders move. Behind Mac, the blast tomato rips further beyond her back. She can continue pushing, but it will only squish Liam into a different position.

Mac is getting frustrated. Her efforts aren't working. Liam still isn't breathing.

Dr. Thelma drops her laser and grabs a scalpel from the tool bag. She moves over to the side opposite of Dr. Ophelia. From there, she starts cutting at the base of the blast tomato to open a second slit. Dr. Molly sees what Dr. Thelma is doing and grabs a third scalpel. She starts cutting at a third location along the base of the bulbous growth. They are perforating the edge.

Mac is isolated from the sound of the outside. She no

longer sees light flashing in the blast tomato, but she doesn't understand what is happening above. *Has Dr. Thelma stopped laser ablation?*

Mac grabs the freeze probe and starts re-freezing a shell above Liam. She also freezes above herself. This time, she wants to cover more area. She wants to cover most of their bodies, if she can. As she sprays, the cooling starts affecting her hand. Her fingers are losing blood flow. Sensation is leaving her fingertips. She keeps pressing the button.

Dr. Molly is becoming frantic. She doesn't want to lose the Morris kids. This has turned out to be more dangerous than she expected, and it is taking longer than expected. Her heart rate is soaring. She is slashing, not simply cutting, with her scalpel. For a brief second, she loses focus and thinks, *in this foreign landscape, I feel like an astronaut with a gashing scalpel. She runs to the opposite side to start perforating the edge.*

Mac's dome is forming. As one side freezes, she returns to re-freeze her already completed portions, but she is progressively making a larger and larger solid surface.

Breathing is tough. Mac is coughing and choking on a liquid from the blast tomato. She has no way to prevent it from seeping into her mouth and nose. When splatter hits her eyes, all she can do is blink in the hopes that it clears her vision just enough to keep working.

In a snap decision, Mac decides that she is done freezing. She drops the freeze probe at her side.

Lift with your legs, she thinks. From the prone position, Mac uses all the strength in her quads to lift the blast tomato with her butt in a pushup. She forms a wedge with her knees bracing the weight. With the added room, she rolls her palms back toward her side. She takes in a huge breath and starts pushing with her palms. This is the most difficult pushup she has ever performed. As weight leaves Liam's body support, it becomes even heavier. Mac lets out a loud roar.

The base of the bulbous growth starts to rip. The perforation is working.

Mac feels her strength building. It is becoming easier. Her elbows are getting closer to locked position. Her back is freezing from the cold surface, but she barely notices with the burning rush of adrenaline in her biceps.

As the perforation keeps ripping, it starts a chain reaction. The more it rips, the easier it becomes to rip. One side pops out of the red net and leans toward Dr. Molly. She drops her scalpel and jumps up to grab the hanging forceps. When Dr. Molly's weight is added, it wrenches the blast tomato free on the opposite side.

Mac locks her elbows, then lifts her butt higher, bringing her knees off the ground and forming a downward dog. It's getting lighter. The momentum of the blast tomato is lifting it away from her. She drops back to her knees, releases from the matter above her and picks her palms off the ground. Mac finds the space above her to push straight up from her knees. She forms punching fists and jams them upwards toward the blast tomato. It releases from the red net and flips out to the side of Dr. Molly.

Liam and Mac are free from underneath the growth. Mac can breathe again. Despite the air, Liam cannot.

Mac collapses from exhaustion. She falls to her brother's side, oblivious to the world around her. Her vision goes dark.

33

Dr. Thelma jumps into the crater and pulls Mac to the surface. Dr. Ophelia does the same with Liam. Dr. Molly gets pinned by the overturned blast tomato but wiggles free.

Mac lets out a gasp for air. Her eyes open and she sees Dr. Thelma's face looking straight at her.

"Liam!"

Dr. Thelma puts her fingers to Mac's throat. She is staring at her wrist watch. "Shhhh," she says.

"Staff assist!" shouts Dr. Ophelia.

Dr. Molly rushes to her side.

Mac tries to sit up to see her brother, but Dr. Thelma keeps her pinned down. Mac breathes in deeply. Dr. Thelma shakes her head disapprovingly and Mac knows to stay still.

"200!" shouts Dr. Thelma.

Mac can feel blood rushing back to her limbs. Her feet start to tingle. Her right hand is still frozen from the freeze probe.

"Defib," Dr. Ophelia says to Dr. Molly.

"180!" shouts Dr. Thelma. "Dropping!"

There's a split second of processing. Fomacula is silent.

Mac can't tell if anybody is breathing. Dr. Thelma moves her head and looks toward Dr. Ophelia. Mac gets a glimpse of the hole above them. The sky through the hole is a pale blue with a tint of green.

"160!" shouts Dr. Thelma.

"Code blue!" Dr. Ophelia shouts back.

Dr. Thelma sets Mac's head down. "Stay," she says. Then she rushes to the side of the other doctors. Mac is left all alone, laying in the red net, staring through the hole. She feels useless with Liam unconscious and not breathing. *What have I done?*

"Defib," Dr. Ophelia says.

Mac hears some shuffling. A bag is unzipped.

Mac's eyes close. Her arms are limp. She thinks she hears heavy breathing. Maybe CPR.

Mac jolts awake with the sound of a shock to Liam's system. *Oh no*, she realizes. She sits up. The world is spinning from the blood rushing out of her head. She sees sparkles in the foreground of her vision. *How long was I out?*

"Clear!" Dr. Ophelia says.

There's a *thu-thunk* sound.

Mac's vision is still blurry as she springs to her feet. She tries to rush over to Liam, but she can't find a straight line.

"Still nothing," Dr. Molly says.

Mac's vision returns. She sees her little brother on the ground, lifeless. The doctors are around him. She wells up in tears, but her throat is too dry to make a sound when she tries to cry out.

Thu-thunk

Dr. Molly puts her hand back at Liam's throat. "Got something!"

The doctors hold their breaths and stare at Liam in hopes that he will let out a breath of his own.

1 second passes.

Dr. Thelma glances at Mac. Her eyes are warning the

girl to stay back. Mac knows not to interrupt the professionals as they do their work. She wants nothing more than to help but also knows any attempt would only distract the doctors.

2 seconds pass.

Dr. Molly brushes Liam's forehead free of hair. His eyelids are shut, and his face has turned a pale color

3 seconds pass.

Dr. Ophelia sets down the defibrillator to go back in for CPR.

Liam lets out a giant gasp for air. His eyes open to the world.

Mac collapses to the ground, overcome with emotion. Her little brother is breathing again. She can't look at this point.

She hears Liam's words through her own tears.

The doctors check Liam's vitals.

They ask him questions.

He is responding.

This is the closest that Mac has ever been to seeing death. She certainly hasn't seen it in her own family. The emotional toll is immense. Her cheeks are whimpering in relief.

Liam is confused. He has no recollection of events. He remembers hiking and getting stung by a bee, but doesn't know where he is, when the doctors ask him. They tell him to lay down for a few minutes.

The doctors continue to monitor Liam's progress. They ease back to calm as he begins to recover. His blood pressure returns to normal. Liam's heart rate and breathing also return to normal. He is allowed to get up.

Dr. Molly jumps down into the crater and starts cleaning the mess. She cuts away bits of blast tomato that hang onto the red net surface. This isn't the type of job that you can do 95%. She knows that the entirety of the blast tomato must be removed.

Mac regains her composure. She wipes her eyes free of tears and stands up to greet her little brother. They are both covered in a blood-red liquid.

"Are you okay?" Mac asks.

"I think so."

"I thought we lost you. I thought I lost you."

"Here I am."

"Seeing your face, hearing your voice—"

"Are you okay?" Liam asks. "You look flabbergasted."

"Just flummoxed," Mac replies.

She pulls his body into her own. Every time Liam inhales, his diaphragm gives a slight push against her torso, a reminder that her brother is alive. Her nostrils flare and her jaw sinks, but she can't help but crack a little smile with tip of her lip.

34

"The sky is clear," Liam says.

"Thanks to you, little brother," Mac says.

The Morris kids are walking back toward Ivv with the doctors. Mac looks up through the red leaves mimicking the red sky. The year was coming to an end. The day was coming to an end. Her adventure was coming to an end.

Snick also turns around and walks toward Ivv. Her path back may be lonelier, but it is no less triumphant.

"And you too, Spectra," Dr. Molly adds, forgetting the nickname. "You did a great thing today."

Spectra has never liked the attention, but she was pleased that her efforts had not gone without recognition of some kind.

"Look!" Liam points. "You can see the moon through the trees too."

The swallows in the canopy are chirping. The sound of the forest rings harmoniously with the clearer sky. Crunchy leaves resonate sound off trunks of birch. A light wind whistles through the branches of the ash trees.

The sky, Mac thinks. *It's later than I realized.*

"What time is it?" Mac asks Dr. Thelma.

The answer is expected, but it isn't pleasing. Mac

realizes they will be late for dinner. There is no avoiding admitting that they snuck out of the house. Their parents will already know.

"Yeah," Liam says. "I'm hungry."

Mac rubs Liam's mop hair. "We'll get some food for you. It was a lot of work out there and you need to regain your strength."

Liam considers arguing that he is still strong, but instead says "Pizza. Pizza will help me."

I was thinking something more like soup, Spectra thinks.

"Did Mom and Dad say what was for dinner?"

"No, but hopefully it's pizza."

"Hey, why don't you tell the doctors what the volume of pizza is."

Spectra had taught Liam a limerick about pizza. It became his favorite and he loved to recite it. He still doesn't even understand what "volume" means, but he loves the rhyme.

Liam recites the poem.

I ordered a pizza that had depth A
Filled with deep dish tomato paste purée;
With radius Z
Topped with pepperoni,
The volume was Pi*Z*Z*A

Poselem and Negelem are still outside playing music when the CAPA Team passes by. They just give a friendly nod in recognition, and don't strike up a conversation. Mac smiles as Negelem plays a sad lullaby.

As Mac grabs the Magic Sled of Nir, Dr. Ophelia says, "What you did really was magic, Macaroon Ravenclaw."

Mac deflects and says, "Any sufficiently advanced magic is indistinguishable from technology."

"You too, Snickerdoodle Hufflepuff," Dr. Ophelia adds.

Both Spectras ride their sleds through the Couplera

Gate and recombines into a single Spectra.

The rest of CAPA team walks right through. Liam's fingers feel the metal surface as he passes.

"Huh," says Dr. Molly. "I just thought of something."

"What's that?" asks Spectra.

"Your power, the ability to see beneath the surface, reminds me of this ophthalmic technique called Optical Coherence Tomography."

"What's *that*?" asks Spectra.

"So, an interferometer is an optical tool that compares the minute differences between a reference arm and a sample. It's incredibly precise. You get details on the order of the wavelength you are using. It can be smaller than the wavelength, in fact. And wavelengths of light are tiny. In OCT, a patient's eye acts as the sample."

Spectra is intrigued. She doesn't quite understand, but she finds it captivating.

"Historically, scientists used a laser to create an interferometer," Dr. Molly continues, "but if you use a wide-band source like a near infrared superluminescent diode, you can separate the wavelengths with a spectrometer to get depth. That depth is what I mean. That's like how you can see through the layers of tissue."

"It's pretty much magic," says Dr. Thelma.

"Oh yeah," says Dr. Molly.

"I've seen that used to detect retinoblastomas," Dr. Thelma says. "Those are like pediatric eyeball cancer. Ophthalmologists can restore vision and save children's lives."

"That's straight fire!" Liam says.

"It really sounds like magic," Spectra says.

"It's just good science and engineering," Dr. Ophelia says.

"Maybe magic isn't properly defined," says Dr. Thelma.

"Magic isn't magical to a magician," says, Dr. Molly. "It could be that magic is just doing something that others can't explain."

Harry Potter was a scientist? Spectra thinks. *Are engineers just wizards without wands?*

The doctors pause to think about the definition of magic.

"And those kids are incredibly lucky to live in an era when eye doctors have such incredible devices," adds Dr. Molly.

"Have you used one?" asks Dr. Ophelia.

"I used one in a wet lab once," Dr. Molly says, "but I haven't got to use one on an actual patient yet. Can't wait 'til we get one."

"Don't need it," says Dr. Ophelia. "When you have experience like I do."

"No amount of experience will let you see below the epithelial layer of the retina."

Dr. Ophelia groans. She knows she needs the new device. She has to keep up with modern trends as younger doctors like Dr. Molly adopt new technology and attract more patients. "Just give me a good microscope."

"You can get an attachment that interfaces with the microscope you already have."

Dr. Ophelia has nothing left to say. She knows she has no good reason to avoid a tool that is so critical to patient health.

"And Spectra," Dr. Molly adds, "as we were talking about eyes, I remembered that I needed to tell you something."

"What's that?"

"You mentioned Sinister and Dexter earlier."

"The book did, but yes."

"In our field, we use 'Sinister' to denote 'left' and 'Dexter' to denote—"

"Let's not put ideas in her head," Dr. Ophelia interrupts.

"I'm fine," Spectra says. She considers the implication of the terms.

"I'm not," Liam says. "I'm hungry."

"We're almost back to Ivv, Liam," says Spectra. "We'll go get you some food."

"Pizza. Can we have pizza please?"

35

Where does one go when the task is complete?
She knew who she was, but who will she be?
Beyond the mission and drive to compete,
She deserves at least to eat a cookie.

What's left of the clouds in the dimming sky are moving from West to East with considerable pace. When Spectra left that morning, there had not been much wind. Now there is. The cool breeze nips at Spectra's ears, turning them red and cold.

Spectra knows that she will be in trouble when she gets back home. She and Liam are late for dinner, and they are covered in the red fluid from the blast tomato. Ruby and Hugh will know immediately that they have been out. Her only hope is that they are happier without the fog and that her accomplishment generates some empathy.

The fall colors of Ivv seem more vibrant. The fog had been damping their effect. Spectra smells some pumpkin spice, cinnamon, and apples in the distance. She smells smoke too, but actual smoke from a fire pit, not the sinister fog.

The crisp weather makes her happy. She loves October.

It's a month for playoff baseball and big football games. It's a month for Ray Bradbury and Tim Burton. It's a month for flannel and scarves and vests. And from now on, Spectra will always associate October with something in her hand as well, the Magic Sled of Nir. *Maybe I'll need this next year*, she thinks.

The village of Ivv is like a camera sensor. Spectra will visit each house to trick-or-treat come Halloween night. Each house will be like a pixel of that camera, viewing her costume, and then supplying a signal output. In the case of Ivv, that signal output will be candy. The more excited the homeowners are to see her costume, the more generous they will be with sugary snacks.

The houses are going to see a lot of kids that night. The ones in the center of town usually have the best candy. She can get full-size candy bars in the good parts of town. On the edges, she'll pass teenage boys dressed in devil horns, pulling pranks and causing mischief. The candy won't be as good on the edges of Ivv.

If Spectra hadn't removed the fog from Ivv, she doesn't know if anybody would be excited enough to give candy. They might have all decided Halloween was no longer fun. In that sense, the village would have been like an unplugged camera. If there's no power to the pixels, they don't get excited, and Spectra would get no treats.

As she sees door after door, she realizes just how many lives she has improved. Her accomplishment will bring clarity and happiness to all of Ivv.

Engineers don't follow their dreams. They follow test results down unknown paths to wherever they may lead. The act of science is an adventure, filled with just as much mystery as any fantasy story, only the scientist must solve each mystery.

Spectra likes this about engineers.

To be on the edge of the known world, she thinks, *exploring mysteries and solving problems, that would be the kind of adventure I could sign up for as an adult.*

She had never considered the career path before, but when Dr. Molly said that stuff about magic and science, Spectra was captivated with the idea. She knows that she can't actually grow up to be a ninja or a wizard, and she's only a couple years away from college, when she will have to be serious about planning for a career. She decides to consider the idea more.

Spectra ages a little bit every time she slices off possibilities of who she could be. For a while, it's nice. It builds structure, focus. At each toll gate, she pays the price of discipline. Great things can only be accomplished by paying this toll. But by adulthood, others will define her by the things she has done, by the sum of her accomplishments. She will define herself by her sacrifices, necessary as they are on her way to the accomplishments. The two definitions of the adult she becomes will rarely see eye to eye.

"That was quite the adventure," Dr. Molly says.

"It has been great working with you," Dr. Thelma says.

Dr. Ophelia nods in agreement. She breaks into a half-smile.

"I couldn't have done it without your help," Spectra says. "I know because I tried to do it all by myself first!"

Dr. Molly laughs. "You can do a lot of amazing things all by yourself, Spectra. I've seen how you work. You have a bright future ahead of you. But some tasks are too big for just one person."

"It was quite lucky, what we—," Dr. Ophelia says.

"Quite *magical*," Spectra corrects.

"Yes," says Dr. Ophelia, "I suppose so."

"Come on, Spectra," Liam says. "I'm hungry."

Spectra looks at her little brother and her heart melts. He risked his life to go on an adventure with her.

"We probably should get back," Spectra says. "Our

parents are probably worried sick about us."

The doctors say goodbye to the Morris kids.

Spectra puts her arm around Liam's shoulders. They turn toward home.

36

"Where have you been?" Hugh says, opening the front door.

There's no point in lying, but the truth will sound like a lie.

"I needed Liam for something very important," Spectra says. "This is my fault."

"You were grounded," Hugh says. "How did you even— Where— What was so important that you needed to sneak out of the house with your brother?"

"We got rid of the fog."

"Spectra."

"We did, Dad," Liam says.

Hugh turns toward Liam. It softens his tone.

"You have to believe us," Spectra says.

Ruby approaches from inside the house. Her face shows visible disgust. "Hugh, whatever it is you are arguing about, let's clean off the kids first and then discuss it, please."

Hugh's eyes meet Ruby's. "Fine," he says.

Spectra and Liam are let into the house to shower off. They put their clothes directly into the washing machine. Spectra finds a spot in the garage to store the Magic Sled of Nir.

Hugh is a big fan of Ray Dalio, the hedge fund manager of Bridgewater Associates. Ray runs his frim with the principle of radical transparency. He espouses the idea that it is much better to know your flaws and try to fix them than to manage without sincere input. He wants to know what he's doing wrong so that he can start doing things right.

Ruby appreciates that Hugh is able to take the constructive criticism. A couple years ago, she noticed that he was struggling to keep his inactivity time to below 23.5 hours per day, and when he wasn't at work, he was mostly on the couch. She calmly sat down with him and suggested that he should find some outdoor hobbies. Hugh took the suggestion and acted. He bought a bike first. He started riding it around Ivv to get some exercise. He couldn't ride very long because he got tired quickly. Then he picked up a second activity, one that got him outside more, but wasn't as tiring. He started gardening. With the two new hobbies, he became visibly happier, and Ruby was thankful.

Ruby is radically transparent with Hugh about the kids sneaking out of the house as well. She tells him to go easy on the kids, because they may have done what they claim. High doesn't believe it, but he trusts the judgement of his wife, and decides not to go harsh.

First-time parents are often overly worried about everything. They will go out of their way to protect their children. They will buy any item that claims to be safe. They will feel guilty about anything safe they don't buy. When other parents take a precaution, they feel they must compete. Then a second child comes along. They realize that the kids will be just fine. Their standards get relaxed and they stop helicopter parenting.

Hugh finds some blame in himself for not watching Spectra closer. *What did she do all day?*

He is also able to find nuance in the situation. He knows that we innately judge ourselves by our intentions and others by their actions. He doesn't want to fall into that trap. *Whether or not she did what she said, what did Spectra intend?*

Hugh takes this sentiment into account. He cares deeply for his daughter and understands that she will have innumerable difficulties in life. He tries to see things from her perspective. Her courage is admirable. She is an achiever, even if also a *mischiever*.

Spectra sits down on the couch. She is all clean.

The smell of soup fills the house with joy. Liam is in the kitchen with Ruby, trying to get dinner before everybody else.

There's an uncomfortable silence as Spectra waits for her punishment. Hugh is holding that silence for effect and to collect his thoughts and composure.

"Was it dangerous?" he finally asks.

It's not the question she was expecting.

"Liam almost died," she says.

Hugh pulls his hand to his mouth. He believes his daughter about this.

"I had to climb in and save him. And then the doctors had to revive him."

"He looks alright now."

"He's pretty resilient. I was a mess of emotions."

"The doctors…"

"Dr. Ophelia, Dr. Thelma, and Dr. Molly. They are pretty much heroes."

"Hmmm…"

"It's a long story, but there was this blast tomato in Fomacula, which was this weird place at the end of a path. Refarm was at the end of another path. I found a sled after reading a book, and then found a gate too. That's where Liam almost died. Under the blast tomato, I mean."

Spectra specifically left out the word "magic." She

knows that her dad wouldn't believe her if she said it.

"It sounds like quite the adventure," Hugh says.

"It really was."

"That still doesn't explain why you felt you had the right to sneak out of the house. Even for saving the town, you have to follow the rules, Spectra."

"I know."

"We're going to eat soup as a family tonight," Hugh says. "We can celebrate your adventure during dinner."

Spectra perks up.

"But after dinner, you are grounded again. And none of that sneaking-out-grounded stuff. Actually-staying-in-your-room-grounded."

"Okay."

"You are going to make up for the time that you missed while you were out of the house, and then I'm going to tack on an additional night for breaking the rules."

The punishment wasn't as harsh as Spectra had worried it would be.

Hugh smiles. "Now, let's go get some soup."

37

Most of the towns in Tuscany removed their rampart walls, but the town of Lucca kept and maintained its wall. Lucca found a use for the wall beyond military protection. There's a pedestrian promenade on the wall with parks and trees. Bikes circle the walled city on sunny days.

When Hugh was younger, he rented a bike to ride around the Lucca wall. As he circled the city, he noticed that parts of the wall were different, but it was much more noticeable to see changes looking not at the wall itself, but at the town contained within its embrace. On top of the wall were rows of perfectly planted trees, parks for relaxing, and even a restaurant, but most of the pathway was similar enough to other parts that it felt unworthy of notice. Looking inside the wall, however, he noticed churches and palaces and parks and restaurants and colorful flowers adorning verandas on top of beautiful old houses.

In life, Hugh had not paid much attention to his own path. He saw trees and parks, just like on the wall, but the immediate infinitesimal changes were unworthy of note. It was only as he saw his daughter growing into a woman that he felt his own age. Each year of life was like a circle around Lucca: pleasant, but similar enough to the last trip around as to be missed.

Spectra was trying to avoid the rut of fate, but her own paths are rarely as illuminating as the one she took to Fomacula and Refarm. Although her life was changing far faster than her father's, she also had a difficult time noticing the roll of the calendar.

She looks toward Liam to notice life changing. They are both growing, both circling the sun one year at a time, but she pays attention to the way her brother changes. The choices she makes seem normal, expected, and planned. And why not? They are on her path. But Liam's choices seem curious, as she sees them from afar. Her own actions rarely surprise her, but the strange actions of her brother on a different path often do.

Life can be like that. Whether struggling to find adventure in life, like Hugh, or captivated by so much adventure that it feels constraining to not have it, like Spectra, it feels like rounding the wall in Lucca. It feels like the path to Refarm, unnoticeable and unimportant until compared to the path to Fomacula. Only in comparing the two was Spectra able to see the tiny details.

Whether riding a bike or climbing a trail, what's on a different path is far more noticeable than what's directly ahead.

Hugh grounded his daughter, but he is thrilled to see her budding independence on this trip around the sun.

Spectra doesn't have a job; she's still just a kid. She knows that she won't get to choose who hires her, only who she applies to work for. She won't get to choose her role, only how she presents herself as an adult.

In the meantime, she gets to decide who she wants to be. That's why she gets enamored with being a ninja or wizard, because she gets to choose how to present herself fully. While still a kid, nobody can keep that persona from becoming all-encompassing. Tomorrow she might decide to become a doctor or an engineer, but today she is happy to live in a world filled with magic.

She's happy to play the part as she thinks it should be played. She knows that a responsible ninja must pick her spots, and this night is not the night for additional mischief.

After dinner, Spectra returns to her room and closes the door. She lays down on her bed and thinks about all that has happened.

It was worth it, she thinks. She always thinks that adventure is worth it. *What else would I do if not seeking adventure?*

Fortunately, the books on her bookshelf contain adventures.

Unfortunately, the walls of her room contain her adventures.

Knock, knock.

Spectra is startled by the subtle sound at her door. *Did I leave something downstairs?*

She walks over to her door and puts her hand on the handle. It feels cold to her palm. She pauses, rather than opening.

Knock, knock.

"Who is it?" she asks.

"It's me," Liam says.

Spectra opens the door slowly. Liam is standing there with a big grin on his face and a hand behind his back.

"Hi," she says.

"I know you are grounded and all," Liam says, "but I wanted to thank you for taking me with you on the adventure today."

A tear forms in Spectra's eye. She knows that it shouldn't mean anything to her to hear her brother appreciate what she did, but the weight of guilt from all the day's failures gets lifted from her gut.

"You're welcome, Liam."

"And for saving my life."

Spectra's throat is closing up at the thought of almost losing her brother. "It was nothing," she says. "Just a little bit of magic."

Liam looks over his shoulder and then back to Spectra. He lowers his voice. "You're not the only ninja in this house, you know."

Spectra looks Liam in the eyes. "Oh yeah?" she says.

Liam pulls his hidden hand out from behind his back. "Would you like a cookie?"

ABOUT THE AUTHOR

Jake Smith was born in Portland, Oregon. He holds a BS in Electrical Engineering from New Mexico Tech and an MS in Optical Engineering from Arizona. Jake currently works as a New Product Introduction Optical Engineer on the Optical Coherence Tomography devices for Leica Microsystems in Raleigh, North Carolina, where he lives with his wife. This is his first novel.